BOAT SONG

BOAT SONG

Frances Ward Weller

MACMILLAN PUBLISHING COMPANY
New York
COLLIER MACMILLAN PUBLISHERS
London

Hunt $5.50 1990

Macmillan Publishing Company
866 Third Avenue, New York, NY 10022
Collier Macmillan Canada, Inc.

First Edition
Printed in the United States of America

10 9 8 7 6 5 4 3 2 1

The text of this book is set in 12 pt. Fournier.

Library of Congress Cataloging-in-Publication Data
Weller, Frances Ward.
Boat song.
Summary: Troubled because he cannot communicate
better with his father, eleven-year-old Jonno finds
unexpected help from a colorful Scottish bagpiper he
meets while visiting Cape Cod.
[1. Bagpipers—Fiction.   2. Fathers and sons—
Fiction.   3. Cape Cod (Mass.)—Fiction]   I. Title.
PZ7.W454Bo   1987   [Fic]   86-12647
ISBN 0-02-792611-7

ACKNOWLEDGMENTS

The story of the piper on the battlements, in Chapter 13, I found in Hope Stoddard's *From These Comes Music* (New York, Thomas Y. Crowell Co., 1952).

I first heard of a piper's role in the Normandy invasion while assisting with research for Cornelius Ryan's *The Longest Day* (New York, Simon and Schuster, 1959).

I am grateful to Anne and Thomas Downs of Madison, New Jersey, for helping me put words in Rob Loud's mouth. And I am much indebted to Gerald F. Stack of Pequannock, New Jersey, for his generous sharing of knowledge and delight concerning the pipes.

BOAT SONG

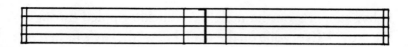

Beyond the bleachers, the sun was setting behind a grove of pines. Great slanting shafts of light between the trees cast golden curtains between Jonno, in center field, and Doug, at second base. The pitcher's mound, where Mickey moved in twilight, seemed as far away as another country.

The light reminded Jonno of storm clouds breaking up on the Atlantic, of the beach he remembered through cold winters, the beach he'd be on, once these championship games were over. He wouldn't mind being there right now, but he'd better forget that. They still had this ball game to win, in order to go on to next week's regionals.

Minutes ago, victory had seemed certain. They'd come into this last half of the ninth inning with a one-run lead and the bottom of the Essex order coming to bat. Mickey had struck out the first two Essex batters, clean and simple. But now, peering through deceptive falls of light, Jonno could see that Mick was starting to tire.

"Come on, Mick. He's no hitter; he's no hitter." Doug's infield chatter drifted back to Jonno. As if in answer, the batter rapped a hard grounder to the third baseman and rocketed down to first base ahead of the throw.

The top of the Essex order was coming up.

"Mickey—Mick! You're lookin' good! Strike him out,

baby; supper's on the table!" A chuckle rippled through the crowd. Everyone on the team knew Mickey's father. A nice man, part cheerleader and part entertainer.

Mick looked weary, but he threw one strike and then another. "Way to go!" His father's cheer sounded loud even from center field. Jonno wondered how Mickey could just grin at the bluster.

Mick's windup looked more and more labored. It was too bad their other strong pitcher was nursing a sore elbow. Ball one. Ball two. Ball three. That runner on first could score even on a long fly ball.

"Mick! Come on, Mick, I wanna go home!"

The bellows from the sidelines made Jonno grateful that his own father was, at least, not a yeller. Not in public, nor even at home, like Doug's father, whose temper was like a summer storm, with flurries of arm waving and gusts of yelling "So what is all this? Who are you, anyway?"—all of which blew over as quickly as they came. Jonno's own father was more like a high-course tide, strong and pre-dictable, threatening to sweep Jonno into a shape he thought appropriate.

"Ball four. Take your base."

So with two out and two on, the second man in the Essex order came to bat. The field and stands were abnor-mally quiet. Jonno squinted against the lightfalls, straining to stay neutrally balanced so that he could be off in the right direction with the crack of the bat.

The batter swung, and a screaming, rising liner flew at Jonno out of the twilight. He had to get that ball to the catcher. He sprinted backward with an eerie sense of run-ning under water. He caught up with the ball as it bounced

2

toward the fence; he had it in his glove. Beyond the curtains of light, the first runner was rounding third. Jonno laid his whole body into the throw to home plate, and it felt like his strongest throw ever.

He watched it head for the plate with disbelief. It was strong, all right, too high and wide for the catcher to handle. Joe did well to get his glove on it at all. Then, in what seemed to Jonno the longest moment of his life, the ball spun up and away from Joe as two runners crossed the plate, to tie and win the game for Essex.

Jubilation erupted in the Essex stands. Leaping and yelling, players from the Essex bench surged toward home plate, where Joe walked in circles, kicking dust. Jonno was aware of teammates drifting off the field, but for another long moment, in sun and dappled shade and shadow, he and Doug and Mickey stood, almost in line, staring toward the plate and the play that might have been.

Doug broke the spell of disbelief. "That could have happened to anyone, Jonno. Hey—Mick!" But Mickey was already heading for the coach's huddle.

"Look, guys." Coach Kluck had his hand on Mickey's shoulder. "I know you're disappointed. I'm disappointed, too, but you should be proud to've come this far. Maybe we all learned some lessons tonight. About how fast a situation can go from good to bad. That a game is never won till it's over. I know you did your best, and that's all any coach can ask for. So be happy, guys, and have a great rest of the summer."

"Mick," said Jonno, "I'm really sorry."

"It's okay." Mick's eyes were wet. "It wasn't you who put those guys on base."

"Jonno." Coach Kluck pounded Jonno's shoulder gently. "That was a tough one. But there'll be other years."

After the handshakes on the field came the parents' turn to commiserate. "Never mind, you guys—we're proud of you!" said Doug's father with unaccustomed calm. "Oh well, Mick," said Mickey's father, clapping him on the back, "I guess we'll feed you anyway."

A little humor didn't hurt, Jonno reflected. He dreaded finding his own father, who wouldn't joke but analyze. Phil Ayres always had to say one thing too many. "He just never quite gets out of the classroom," Jonno's mother once explained. "He has to probe and articulate everything."

His father was alone, tall and commanding, waiting by the car. From the way his hair stood on end, Jonno could tell he had been pretty excited.

"Too bad, kiddo," he first said quietly.

"Where's Mom?"

"She went ahead to start supper," his father said as he started the engine. "Since you're finished with baseball, we can leave for Gram's day after tomorrow, and your mother wanted to get a head start on the packing marathon."

"Will Gram be ready for us?"

"She said yesterday she'll be glad to see us whenever we can get there."

"Did she happen to say if Peter Baldwin's around yet?" Trying to prolong the neutral conversation, Jonno cheered himself up a little. Sailing and swimming and biking with Peter had livened up a lot of days in past summers.

"She didn't say," his father answered. Jonno could hear impatience in his voice. "Look, Jonno, before we get home you need to do some thinking about what happened out there tonight."

Jonno felt his throat closing with familiar frustration. Did his father really suppose he wasn't thinking about it? "I'm sorry I messed up, Dad," he said as calmly as he could. "I think I feel a lot worse about it than you do."

"Jonno, I'm not trying to make you feel worse, and it's not a question of how I feel. You know I'm not one of those fathers with my whole ego tied up in what you do in a game."

That was true, Jonno thought. His father had no problem with self-respect.

"My point is, there's one good thing about mistakes— you can learn from them. You're too good an athlete to let this sort of thing happen without analyzing it. Now it seems to me that when the game was nearly over, you let down a little, and then when the adrenaline started flowing, you overreacted. Just because you'd let down a little. What do you think?"

"I don't know, Dad!" Jonno could feel his voice and temper rising. "Anybody can make a mistake!"

"But you're an exceptional person, Jonno, not an 'anybody.' And what makes a champion is coming through in the clutch. Hemingway said it better. 'Grace under pressure.'"

That was true, too, and Jonno knew it. He just didn't need to have it thrown at him right now.

"Dad, I hate looking like a fool out there, and I hate letting everybody down, so I don't need a lecture." He was choking now, in an undefined muddle of grief and anger. "Can we just drop it?"

His father's jaw stiffened as he swung the car into the driveway. "Damn it, Jonno, I was only trying to help."

That was it. All very civilized, with no waving arms and no "Who are you, anyway?"—but also with no sunshine after the rain. Jonno was simply dropped like a stubborn bit of flotsam left for the next high tide. "Let him eat in the TV room," his father told his mother. "He wants to be left alone."

"Tough luck, darling," said his mother, bringing him a heaping plate of his favorite macaroni casserole, fragrant with garlic and tomatoes, a vat of salad, and a pitcher of milk.

"Not luck, Mom," he said bitterly. "An obvious lack of 'grace under pressure.'"

"Oh, Jonno." His mother looked as if she might cry. "You know he just wants everything to go right for you."

"Thanks, Mom." Suddenly he was fiercely hungry. "He's right about one thing. I'd rather not talk about it."

So she gave him a quiet hug and two desserts. They got him through the evening. But he'd have to get himself through the memory of causing his team to lose the game, and the prospect of setting out on vacation with his father angry at him.

"Haarrhhh! Haarrhhh! Haarrhhh!" Through cupped hands Jonno breathed a crowd's roar like a sound of distant surf. "Now coming to the plate for the Yankees, in the bottom of the eighth, the shortstop, Sparky Mazaratti. *Haarrhhh!* He's batting .305, sports fans, and this could be the Yankees' inning. The Sox took a commanding lead with four runs on a grand slam in the top of the seventh, so the Yanks must rally in the clutch to pull out this crucial game."

"Haarrhhh!" Jonno lowered the fist he'd been holding before him like a microphone and shook the dice onto the gameboard again. "Whooo!"

The yelp made Pippin lift his sleepy head from Jonno's bare foot.

"Hey, Pip." The golden retriever opened one brown eye as Jonno scratched the top of his head. "You're my buddy, aren't ya? It's just too bad you can't roll dice."

Pippin's tail thumped the floor as footsteps sounded on the stairs at the end of the long porch.

"Jonathan Ayres, you are getting weirder and weirder!" His sister Kate peered at him from the top of the steps. Kate was never one to mince words, thought Jonno, as she stalked toward him, carrying a bulging bag from the drugstore. Stocking up on beautification supplies to take to

Gram's cottage. Working on a model's saunter, trying to look tall.

The truth was that if he stood he'd be looking down at Kate, even though she was two years older. Being overgrown might explain his recent problems with real baseball. He'd overheard his parents often enough. "Jonno's in another phase of gross motor activity." "I can't wait till his coordination catches up with the size of his feet."

"Aren't you ever going to outgrow make-believe?" Typically Kate persisted, like Pip with a bone. "It's bad enough when you sit out here huffing and mumbling over that dumb game with Doug, but doing it alone sets a new record for weirdness!"

Jonno leaned back and the old wicker chair protested faintly. "We try," he said with as much dignity as possible, "to simulate actual game conditions. The noise of the crowd is part of the atmosphere. Which you wouldn't know, since instead of doing something healthy like following the current sports scene, you are always boogying around your room with the Rolling Wrecks going full blast!"

Kate hated to be outtalked, so Jonno purposely hurried on while her mouth was open to reply. "And one of the best things about this game," he added, "is that you can play it alone if you want to."

Kate threw up her hands, bag and all. "Why would anyone want to play anything alone?"

"Well," said Jonno, "it sure beats the company that's usually available around here."

Kate flushed. "Don't dump on me, Jonno, just because you're down about losing a baseball game!"

"The problem's just you, Kate," he lied.

"Oh no, it's not!" Fleetingly Kate's bony face looked almost sympathetic. But when she turned on her heel, her shrug spoke her mind: Nobody could understand an eleven-year-old brother.

"Jonno's out on the porch sounding like a storm sewer again," she bellowed to no one in particular as she disappeared through the kitchen door. A burst of sound from the kitchen radio announced that she had reached the shelf by the sink.

"Haarrhhh! Haarrhhh!" He ought to see how this game turned out, but as usual, Kate, small as she was and daffy about rock music, had managed to make him feel self-conscious. "It's not fair, Pip," he muttered. "Sometimes I think you're the only one in the family I'm really related to."

He couldn't help liking his old baseball board game any more than he could help having a perfectly functional anklebone that creaked whenever he walked around barefoot. His mother always told him he would laugh someday when Kate said he reminded her of the clock-swallowing crocodile in Peter Pan, but so far he hadn't found it funny.

He saw nothing funny about his anklebone or his sound effects. Lots of things in the Ayres household were harder to understand than his habits. Even his own name, Jonathan—chosen, his mother said, to be romantic and inspiring. He was thankful his little sister had found it a toddler's tongue-twister and shortened it to Jonno. By the time he could change it legally, his father might have given up teaching English to be a columnist for *Jazz Encore*, his favorite magazine; his mother might be a professional choir director, touring the world very fast to catch more than one Sunday in a week; Kate would be a rock star or a groupie, and Alison a mad pianist. And he would be just plain John, the center fielder or archaeologist or forest ranger, which would be a big relief.

Inside, a door slammed and a low, rhythmic thumping started. Clearly Kate had arrived in her room to begin packing.

"It's everyone else around here that's off the wall," Jonno muttered to himself. He stretched and stood up to survey the driveway. It didn't look at all promising. Less like an organized departure for vacation than like a three-family garage sale, or a neighborhood being evacuated in dire emergency. That was because his father refused to put anything in the back of the station wagon until he had everything grouped according to size and order of importance. "Checking the cargo," his father called it.

Jonno sank back into the slouchy cushions of the wicker chair and closed his eyes. On this one day of the year, he could appreciate his father's problems. One especially exasperating vacation eve, Phil Ayres had said he felt just like General Eisenhower trying to organize D-Day. Packing the car was hardly as challenging as landing troops from four countries on three French beaches one June day toward the end of World War II. But considering the amount of junk everyone thought was needed to go to Gram's, Jonno couldn't blame his father for falling back on his own navy experience to cope with the confusion.

When the car was full and Dad was lashing together the pyramid of extras that rode on the roof, someone always remembered some bulky thing with fourteen corners. Kate could be counted on to smuggle in eighteen kinds of shampoo and lip glop, bushels of stuffed animals and tapes, and last year even her stereo with infuriating skeins of speaker wire.

In the midst of such aggravation, Jonno could see why his father dusted off his choicest navy language as well as his navy knots for dealing with the motley cargo. Sheepshanks, timber hitches, fisherman's bends—the knots' names were nearly as colorful as the shipmates Dad remembered: Snively and Snitko, two tough bosun's mates who specialized in rescuing their buddies from barroom brawls; Haskell Everett Parsley, a boy from the Southern hills who put pebbles in his shoes to make them feel like country roads; and a crowd of others Jonno had heard about ever since he was old enough to listen to stories. Phil Ayres collected favorite characters from real life just as he collected favorite characters from the books and plays he taught so eloquently. They were permanently pinned like specimen butterflies in the showcase of his father's memory.

It bothered Jonno, transforming people into conversational curiosities. Maybe that was because he felt like a specimen himself, under scrutiny, every time he had a confrontation with his father.

Pippin brought him back to the present with a noisy sigh and a whimpering fit that suggested he was dreaming of scaring off a herd of elephants.

A moment later came his father's voice. "Jonno, do I have everything here you need to take?"

Don't mumble, thought Jonno, and don't answer so abruptly that you sound rude. He opened his eyes and looked at his father, who stood with his hands on his hips

11

in the middle of the driveway's chaos. Phil Ayres was wearing a hole-riddled T-shirt and shorts made of sawed-off chinos splotched with layers of black lawnmower oil and dusty pink paint from Alison's woodwork. Checking the cargo, and looking as if he were already shipwrecked.

Just now his father didn't look like anyone's idea of a Renaissance man, though the local paper had declared him one last year in a review of a campus play. "A person of serious competence in varied fields of accomplishment," Jonno found in his dictionary. "Multitalented," said the local paper.

It was true, all of it. And what did a person eleven years old have to say to a Renaissance man? His father had talked to him a lot when he was younger and just a little sponge soaking up fatherly wisdom. Now Jonno felt that Phil Ayres was waiting for him to grow and become worth talking to again—worse yet, that he expected answers Jonno wasn't ready to give. Expert on drama, expert on jazz, expert tennis player, his father was probably happiest, Jonno thought, talking with other experts. Too much always seemed to be expected in a conversation with his father.

"Jonno, did you hear me?" his father called angrily.

Be careful, Jonno thought. "I'm sorry, Dad, I was half-asleep. Everything's there but my baseball game, and the bike if you can carry it with Alison's."

His father tossed his head impatiently. "We may forgo the bikes if we have too much."

"But Dad," Jonno began, "me and Alison wanted—"

"You mean, 'Alison and I,'" his father interrupted.

Right, thought Jonno. Don't argue.

Bursts of overamplified guitar and thuds of bare feet announced that Kate and her first installment of junk were on their way to the launch site. To Jonno's relief, his mother came out the kitchen door. She looked frazzled, but she rumpled his hair affectionately as she watched her husband recoil the lengths of clothesline he used for roof lashings.

Jessica Ayres chuckled. "Well," she said, "I can see that, as usual, what's on the roof will be held together better than any other part of the car!"

Kate pounded onto the porch carrying two suitcases. "Dad," she called as she thumped down the porch steps, "if I can't bring the speakers, can I *pleeease* bring the portable stereo with the tapes?"

"Then I am bringing all my bears!" Eight-year-old Alison bounced through the screen door, back from her piano lesson. "Jonno, I'm done till school starts—five weeks with no practicing, four stickers, and a chocolate bar!"

"Way to go, Al!" For her he mustered up a grin. "Your July went better than mine!"

"I'm sorry about your game." For a minute, her big blue eyes stopped dancing. "Are you still sad?"

Jonno tried to make his eyes as round as hers, and gave her a quick nod.

"Oh, well." She giggled and skipped away. "At least we get to go on vacation sooner."

Jonno sympathized with her impatience. He'd been ready for hours and they wouldn't leave until after midnight, for his father liked to drive when the roads were cool and free. *"Haarrhhh!"* He tossed the dice once more, and just as quickly leaned back again and closed his eyes.

He was ready for wave sounds and windy space. He felt stifled among all these confident performers who talked more than he did, sang as he never could, and were all "tuned in" to something all day long. He felt stifled more by the need to say the right thing to his father.

Even determined little Gram, with all her strong opinions flying, would never turn him into a musician or a great conversationalist. She seemed to find his quietness offensive, and he wasn't looking forward to her interrogations. But her place made up for her prickly personality, for the great Atlantic beach was nearly at her doorstep.

He'd have Pip and Peter. And on the beach, anything could happen. No matter what his father said, on that beach he was an anybody. On the beach, he could just be.

He could smell the sea.

After long, flowing hours on the turnpike when the stars faded and the sky turned from black to gray to icy blue, after slowing down for towns that were the gateways to the sea, there always came a moment that made all the hassle and the hours on the road worthwhile. The view might still be shabby souvenir shops and hamburger stands, but the tang in the air declared the sea was near.

So for the last hour of the trip the sea was a presence, just out of sight. What made everyone else more impatient, cramped, and wriggly for that hour Jonno wasn't sure, but what made him jumpy was the feeling that his favorite spot in the world was waiting for him. His impatience was a little silly, he admitted to himself. The ocean would still be there, whenever he arrived—unchanged, as broad and beautiful as the summer before. Its constancy amazed him.

If he hadn't been so hungry after being up half the night, he would have been willing to forgo the traditional, start-of-vacation breakfast they always ate at the pancake house, before going on to Gram's. But Kate and Alison would never settle for Gram's health cereals and home-made bran muffins. Not after three hundred miles of counting on their annual orgy.

At eight o'clock this first day of August, breakfasters were just trickling into the low-ceilinged rooms cheerful with wood and gingham. The smells of toasting bread, brewing coffee, and warming maple syrup suddenly made eating seem an urgent matter. Jess Ayres chuckled, gazing around their circle of noses bent to menus. "Phil," she said, "it's just as well your mother wouldn't join us. We're not exactly a hotbed of polite conversation."

Every year Gram was invited to meet them for breakfast. But breakfasting at an unpredictable hour was against her principles. "And," she always added with a sniff, "Lord knows what they put in their plastic pancakes!"

Jonno's father shot his wife an amused glance, rubbed his slightly bloodshot eyes, and cast a challenging look around the table. "Well, fellow merrymakers," he said more cheerfully than Jonno thought appropriate to their sleepy state, "*what* are we going to eat this morning—considering Mom's own buttermilk pancakes are second to none and we're not often in a place that offers Belgian waffles and Swiss pancakes laced with chocolate chips?"

"Not to mention French toast and Hawaiian pancakes." Jonno's mother groaned. "My stomach's just as tired as the rest of me, so I'm feeding it a basic mushroom omelet."

"Yum!" Alison's eyes flew from item to item. "Strawberry waffles! Coconut pancakes!" Alison always went for what most resembled dessert. "How can I decide? I know: eeny, meeny . . ."

While both of his parents smiled at Alison, Jonno turned to Kate. She had assumed the dreamy expression she usually reserved for a male rock group that reminded Jonno of a trio of department store mannequins. "Cranberry pancakes!" Kate breathed. "With bacon and extra syrup! I've been planning this for weeks!"

"Coconut!" said Alison triumphantly. "With sausage." Jonno's stomach twinged in protest just thinking about it.

"Well, I'll try the German apple pancakes. Every year I say I will, and now's the time." His father announced it like a challenge and looked right at Jonno. "How about you?"

He would order plain buttermilk pancakes, bacon, and two eggs over easy. Everyone knew he would order plain buttermilk pancakes, bacon, and two eggs over easy.

He looked at his father. "Well, Mom's just having a basic omelet."

"But you're too young to be in a rut," said Phil Ayres, trying to dodge his wife's elbow. "It's important to be willing to try something new. Nothing ventured, nothing gained."

Why did his father make it seem like a dare? Jonno pretended to study the menu curiously, as if it changed from year to year. But vacation was supposed to be for doing what you wanted to do. So when he looked up again and found the waitress at his elbow, he said, "I'll have plain buttermilk pancakes, bacon, and two eggs over easy, please."

Even to himself, it sounded louder than necessary. To cover his embarrassment, Jonno reached for his water goblet. Somehow, as he raised it, its bottom caught his father's glass across the table and sent it teetering toward his father's lap. Phil Ayres's hand shot out, righting his goblet before its rim hit the table. "Oh, well," he said lightly to the waitress who came with extra napkins, "a lapful of ice water is a real waker-upper!"

But between his parents glances flew. His father's look seemed so much nearer hurt than annoyance that Jonno nearly said, "Oh, well, apple." But his mother's look to both of them said, "Let it be."

Though Alison downed her coconut concoctions with the happy little noises of an ecstatic guinea pig, his buttermilk pancakes didn't taste as good as he remembered. Rather flat, like sawdust. Or maybe he was just tired.

Thin sunlight flooded the parking lot as the Ayreses left the pancake house with a fresh bowl of water for Pippin. Warm as it was, the fringes of the sky looked milky, and damp puffs of breeze from the east suggested a chancy sort of day. Jonno knew what his grandmother would say if they grumbled. "You're in New England now, children! If you don't like the weather, wait a minute."

Kate leaped into the backseat ahead of him, and Alison perched on her lap so that there was room for Jonno with the front half of Pip on top of him. Liberated from his cell behind the dog-gate, the big golden retriever huffed expectantly. He's excited, too, thought Jonno. He can probably smell the ocean better than I can.

"Pip, for pete's sake, you're fogging up the window!" Jonno rolled the glass down as his father turned the car away from the center of town onto the beach road.

"I am so glad to get out of that parking lot!" Kate let out an exaggerated sigh. "Everybody stared at us as if we were freaks!"

Her mother chuckled. "It could be because we're carrying everything but the kitchen sink," she replied.

"Nonsense, you disbelievers," said Jonno's father. "They're just admiring my remarkable knots!"

Alison looked at Jonno's unsmiling face. "Will Peter be here?"

Jonno shrugged. "I hope so."

"Don't expect too much from Peter, Jonathan," his mother said gently. "You know, he's more Kate's age than yours."

"Ha!" Kate snorted. "Three months older than I am, if you want to know the truth; he just doesn't look or act it!"

"Now, Kate," said Mom, "some year you may find Peter's turned into a Greek god."

Kate was not amused. "Dad, can't we turn on the radio just long enough to see what the local station is playing this year?"

One benefit of traveling at night was that everyone but Dad slept, instead of debating which radio frequency had the best noise to offer. This was too good an opening to miss.

"Emergency, emergency!" announced Jonno in his best baseball-broadcaster's voice. "Kate Ayres is having withdrawal symptoms! No rock for eight whole hours!"

"Just stuff it, Jonno!" Kate sputtered. "You can't expect us all to live in silence just because you've got the perfect personality for solitary confinement."

Jonno bit back. "If solitary confinement cures insanity, you're the one who needs it."

"Oh, right," sneered Kate. "We're all crazy and you're sane. Doesn't it seem more likely it'd be the other way around?"

"Not all crazy," said Jonno quickly. "Just you."

"Shut up," said Kate.

"Shut up yourself."

Their mother groaned in the front seat.

"Okay, that's enough from both of you," said Dad, in the extremely calm voice he often used just before exploding. "Kate, you got in a couple of low blows, but Jonno, you started it this time." As if to side with Kate, Dad reached over and switched on the radio.

"Oh, wow," cried Kate, easily distracted by a blast of electric guitar. "That's the Endangered Species!"

"Don't I wish," Jonno muttered.

"Just do me a favor and don't boogie while I'm sitting on your knees." Alison leaned forward with her elbows on the back of the front seat, and Jonno peered past her and Pippin at familiar landmarks streaming by. The old cemetery with its wafers of weathered stone. The vegetable stand heaped with butter and sugar corn. The clam bar and the general store.

"'Only yew can share mah space with meee,'" Kate warbled unconcernedly with the radio. Alison hooted on Kate's bouncing knees, and through the din Jonno's father spoke to him, quietly and coolly.

"You know, Jonno, I don't understand how anyone your age can be so stubbornly square."

His mother glanced quickly over her shoulder. "Jonno," she said, "you know he's only half-serious."

But the words were said. And he didn't need to say them, Jonno thought. Even if he suspected that his father sort of scorned him, he hadn't expected him to come right out and say so.

Jonno could think of no reply. He stared silently at fields of wildflowers and little groves of pine. The others were quiet now, too, their excitement growing, each wanting to be first to spy the sea.

A big red barn. A truck garden. On top of the rise, the inn called The Ship's Knees. Around the next curve, where the horizon leaped to infinity, was the Atlantic. Even under this morning's washed-out sky, it held Jonno silent for a long moment. That was all right. He hadn't anything new and interesting to say about the Atlantic anyway. "So square."

His father, never at a loss for words, triumphantly echoed the old whalers. "Thar' she blows!"

"Oh, rats!" cried Alison. "I missed being first again!"

Turning left at the inn onto the narrower road that paralleled the sea, they dipped into hollows lined with shrubs and wildflowers and rose onto knolls with flying glimpses of the water. And at last they turned into a jouncy lane no wider than a driveway, with a grassy center strip and sandy ruts for the car's wheels.

Above the bayberry thickets a wrought-iron goose appeared, wavering in the wind. Pointing toward the bay, Jonno thought automatically. A sea breeze.

"I see the weather vane! I saw that first!" cried Alison, and in a moment there was Gram, bending over a tub of geraniums and straightening a bit stiffly to wave them into the parking space beside the garage.

"Don't mash my nasturtiums!" Gram called militantly, as her son wheeled toward a flower bed. Peppery as ever, Jonno thought, as she tossed aside her trowel to hug Alison, who fell out of the car into her arms.

Pippin scrambled over Kate and took off after a squirrel.

Kate followed with a squawk and a dramatic hobble, as Phil Ayres unfolded himself from behind the wheel and kissed his mother.

"Well, Mama, how's this for shattering your peace? Bodies popping out of all foah doahs!" He loved to tease Gram about her Down East accent.

"Gram, is it supposed to rain? Is it a good beach day?" Alison jumped up and down.

"I haven't the foggiest, Alison, and if you ask me, the weatherman hasn't either. If you don't like the weather, wait a minute!" said Gram, as if on cue. "Well, Kate, how pretty you look! Jess, you must be done in. And Jonno, my word"—except that Gram said "wuhd"—"you're taller than I am, all of a sudden! And how are you otherwise?"

"Oh, fine, Gram," he answered. So square, he thought.

She peered up at him sharply. "Still keeping that *A* average?"

Jonno shrugged.

"Half a year of no letters makes one wonder, you know, but never mind, young man, I'll catch up with you later!"

That sounded like another conversation where too much would be expected. Once you've raised a Renaissance man, Jonno thought glumly, any other boy is bound to be a disappointment. So he hugged her quickly and stood on one foot and then the other, while everyone seemed to mill around and talk without listening. Back up the lane and over the bluff was where he wanted to be. Just to be sure his spot was still the same. Just to make his arrival official.

Pippin bumbled around the corner of the garage, narrowly missing Gram's flower border, and Jonno had an inspiration. "Mom, Dad—could I take Pip over to the inlet, just to get his bounces out?" If he could go off alone for a while before Alison finished her inspection of Gram's cookie jar and game cupboard, maybe he could get the kinks out of his spirit, too, and run off the sting of his father's comment.

Phil and Jessica Ayres gave one another the familiar "what-do-you-think?" look which always made Jonno feel they had ESP.

"It's all right with me," said his father, "but don't be gone too long. We'll want you to get your stuff into the loft and help with settling in."

"And Jonno," his mother added, "that sky's a little threatening. If it starts to get foggy, please don't go onto the outer beach alone."

Before anyone could change his mind, Jonno whipped off his sneakers and socks and started up the lane. They were liberated at last, he and Pip, not just from the cramped car but from shoes and sisters, schedules, and some of the cautions that follow an eleven-year-old person through the year.

Jonno's bare ankle clicked companionably. Here was the tangle of rosa rugosa where he and Alison last met the family of quail. Underfoot the sandy rut felt silky, without the searing heat it would have on a day of blazing sun. When he stepped out of the rut, the grass felt dry and crackly, as it always did here—never moist and thick like the grass at home, but always struggling to rise above the constant sweeps of sand. The trees that stood on this little upland crouched above the cottages. Everything was formed by the ever-sighing wind from the sea.

As they neared the place where the lane crossed the paved road and ran on to the bluff, Jonno found himself moving faster. He called Pip back so they could cross the road safely, and then could wait no longer. By the time he reached the last tall hedgerows that lined the path to the bluff, blocking out everything but the sky, he was heading at a dead run for his annual reunion with the sea.

Jonno burst out of the hedgerow canyon and caught his breath. This was the spot that always felt like a homecoming. He had reached the rim of a bluff that seemed to overlook infinity.

The land fell away steeply in tangles of bayberry, brambles, and rosa rugosa to a cove where boats bobbed at their moorings with the flow of the incoming tide. Forty-two steep wooden steps led down the side of the cliff to the rocky beach below. From there the cove meandered off to the left, past a sandbar that would be covered when the tide was full, and joined the swifter waters of the inlet that led to the town harbor. But straight ahead, across the cove, a long finger of beach stretched northward to the inlet's mouth, and beyond that sandspit was the ocean.

Out there, said Jonno's father, was nothing but water all the way to Portugal. On any clear day the view reached for miles, up the coast and out to sea. Even today, with a screen of fog lying beyond the breakers and hiding the horizon, the sky seemed enormous. Standing here, Jonno felt very small and yet as mighty as the view.

Pippin gave an urgent little groan. He stood at the top of the stairway looking puzzled and impatient, but Jonno wanted to linger and watch the lines of whitecaps ruffling in to shore. From here the waves that towered over ocean swimmers looked small and sounded peaceful. He drank in the great gray bowl of sky and the sea wind that carried the complaints of gulls, the chug of a fishing boat running in before the fog. And something else. An unfamiliar sound without a name.

A wild, high cry came to him in fragments on unsteady puffs of wind from the sea. At first he thought there was someone screaming on the outer beach, but then he realized a person's voice could never call so far. Was it the howl of an injured animal? Or the outcry of a flock of seabirds?

As the sea breeze steadied, Pip stopped wriggling with impatience and came to attention, and Jonno knew suddenly that they heard a melody. As indistinct from here as the fog-hung ocean beyond the lacy line of breakers, but a melody, nonetheless, that rose and fell and echoed itself.

He had never heard anything like it before. The only kind of music he had ever heard on the beach was Kate's kind, the stuff that blared from portable radios propped on blankets. Raucous as it was, that sound was quickly lost in the constant sigh of wind and surf. It wasn't that. There was something strange out there on his beach. Suddenly he couldn't wait to find out what was going on.

"Pip! Come on!"

Jonno plunged down the steep wooden stairs, Pip scuttling behind and hurtling ahead, and began a broken-field run through the little maze of beached sailboats on the cove's rim. Better to watch out for half-buried anchors in the soft sand than to cut his sock-softened feet on the mosaic of mussels and rocks in the harder sand uncovered by the tide. Pip waded into the inlet and swam off after a gull. Deserter, thought Jonno absently, as he pushed himself through the sand. He was panting already! Every summer running on the beach took some getting used to.

He had almost reached the other side of the cove when the wild, singing sound from the outer beach stopped. In its absence all the normal water sounds seemed like silence. Running now under an increasingly chill and leaden-looking sky, Jonno felt the mystery even more. He turned away from the cove and raced across the sandy track laced with beach-buggy treads. He had just struck off onto his favorite path that rose through the grass to the top of the dunes when the music began again. So much closer.

From the top of the dunes he should be able to see what was happening. Even without the lure of a mystery he would be running now, for he loved the first moment of being face-to-face with the Atlantic. He dug in his toes and hurled himself up the dune's crest. But as Pip caught up with him in a shower of cold, briny water, Jonno stopped dead in his tracks with surprise and disappointment.

While he was rounding the inlet, the fog had come ashore. In a soft but treacherous wall, it lay thirty yards ahead of him, all up and down the beach, pushed by the wind, which bit through Jonno's T-shirt now that he stood above the dunes' lee. It hid the ocean and most of the beach, and it was still moving inland. Its edges swirled across the high-water line. And somewhere within the cloud, up the beach to his left, swirled the wild, strange music.

Jonno had run most of a mile after the sound, and he had wanted at least to stick a foot in the ocean, so he could say how cold the water was and how ridable the waves. But there was a family agreement that no one went on the outer beach alone in fog. Today, besides, he had promised his mother. By his silence he had promised. But that wasn't all that kept him on the top of the dune with his hand on Pip's collar.

He was cold not only from the wind. All at once, things seemed not just mysterious but somehow menacing. The fog drifted closer to his dune. The sea pounded dully, insistently, invisibly, its softer sighs and echoes stifled by the fogbank. Or perhaps just overpowered by the wailing, lamenting cry that was coming closer and closer.

What was a banshee? He had probably seen too many of those old British mystery movies where horrors patrolled watery places and lurked in mist. Movies. Why was he thinking of movies about British battles in India?

Steadily the sound came on, moving south along the water's edge just off to his left. Jonno crouched beside Pippin and clutched the dog where the long hair at the back of his neck stood on end. Pip stared into the fog and growled softly. The first tendrils of fog touched the bottom of the dune, and the music washed over them, whirling from a dark place in the mist that Jonno's eyes could barely follow.

The shadow passed below the crest of the beach at a halting pace that matched the dirgelike music. Jonno thought of all the tales of ghosts from shipwrecks off this coast, and shivered. The shadow was fast dissolving into mist again, but still marked by the music. He was torn between wanting to run away and wanting to follow.

But fog drifted now across the dunes toward the cove, and he had promised. So he'd go back to Gram's, but he wouldn't say anything about the sound or the shadow. For what could he say? That on the beach he'd seen a ghost? That in the fog there'd been a wild song that carried all the way from the beach to the bluff? That it was eerie but it drew him all the same?

That was something no one else needed to know. Lots of things happened on this beach that were gone without a sign by the next tide. So maybe he would never hear the sound again.

"It was foggy on the beach," he told his mother. "So we came home."

Surely it was too dark for morning. Sweatshirts, jeans, and Gramp's old sou'wester huddled on hooks across the room, phantomlike in the gloom, marching toward the battered old hatstand that guarded the loft's corner and served as Jonno's closet.

But despite the dimness a phone was ringing somewhere. Jonno rolled over and lifted a corner of the gingham curtain, confirming his suspicions. Yesterday's fog was just a hint of what was coming. On this first full day of vacation it was going to rain. Gram would be dusting off the Chinese checkers board and Alison begging him to play Monopoly, when what he wanted was to scour the beach for the source of yesterday's music.

"Jonno-oh." Alison's three-syllable bellow from the breezeway and the clammy coldness of the floor between the rag rugs woke him up in earnest.

"It's Peter Baldwin, on the phone!" called Alison as soon as Jonno opened the loft door. "He didn't know if we were here yet. He sounds as if he's in a hurry."

Peter always sounded that way, Jonno thought as he padded down to the kitchen. Peter never did anything by halves. Anyone racing a sailboat with Peter had to be ready to win or capsize, and either way Peter laughed about it. If anyone could save this grim-looking day, it was Peter Baldwin.

"Hi, Peter." Jonno leaned against the kitchen wall, partly from sleepiness and partly to shut out the murmur of breakfast conversation raised by Gram and his parents.

"So, Jonno, you're here! How's it goin'?"

"Pretty good." Peter wasn't the sort of person who wanted to hear all your troubles. "I just got up thinkin' this looked like an all-Monopoly day. But I'd sure rather have a catch or hike up the beach until it starts to rain."

There was a curious beat or two of silence before Peter spoke. "I've kind of given up baseball. I'm training for football—in fact, I just got back from running. Want to ride up to Mooncusser Beach after I take a shower?"

That was a twenty-five-mile round trip. "Did you get your ten-speed bike for Christmas?" Jonno asked.

"Yeah. Twelve, actually. How about you?"

"Maybe this year." He'd have to ride his five-speed hard to keep up, but maybe Peter would know something about the music in the fog, and anything was better than inactivity. "Okay, I'll bring some stuff to eat."

"I'll put a Thermos on my rattrap."

"I'll meet you at the end of the Rourkes' driveway?"

There was another pause before Peter answered, but he sounded offhand enough. "No, you get some breakfast, and I'll come on to your house. I'm not sure how long I'll be."

"Okay, Peter. Take it easy."

"Right, Jonno. You stay chilly."

Jonno found himself frowning at the receiver in disbelief. He wasn't even sure what "stay chilly" was supposed

31

to mean, but it sounded suspiciously like some of the things Kate's idols were likely to say at the end of taped interviews. If Peter was trying to turn himself into what Kate considered "a cool dude," he'd scarcely be intrigued by yesterday's shivery adventure. Still, Jonno supposed that really cool dudes didn't suggest bike hikes to Mooncusser Beach.

Pippin was lying in the breezeway as Jonno headed for the outdoor shower, one of the best places at Gram's to think about life. "Stand by," Jonno whispered, lifting one of Pip's floppy ears. "I'm working on our mystery."

He had stuffed a knapsack with a poncho, fruit, and sandwiches and was scraping the last runnels of cereal from one of Gram's blue and white bowls when bike wheels crunched on the gravel driveway. The flying light step was Peter's, all right, but was that really Peter silhouetted against the light in the kitchen doorway?

The rangy figure bent to peer through the screen. "Heyyy, Jonno. Let's boogie!"

It was definitely Peter.

Scrambling to his feet, Jonno found that looking straight ahead gave him a clear view of Peter's Adam's apple. There were the same shock of dark hair and the same cocky, challenging smile, both at least half a foot higher than they were last summer.

"My word, Peter Baldwin, how you have grown!" exclaimed Gram as she hustled in to see who was raising the ruckus.

"Is that Peter Baldwin's voice?" Phil Ayres peered around the fireplace wall that separated living room and kitchen and advanced on Peter with his right hand outstretched, the *New York Times* dangling from his left. Jonno's father looked extraordinarily glad to see Peter, considering the dim view he'd taken of some of Peter's past misadventures. It was an odd scene, Jonno thought. He couldn't recall his father's having shaken hands with any of his friends before.

"My word," said Phil Ayres, "you look terrific, Peter! You look as if you'd spent the winter with a Nautilus machine."

"I'll say." Alison skidded down the last few stairs that led from the dormer room she shared with Kate, and gave Peter the sort of head-to-toe appraisal she might award a visitor from outer space. "Boy," she blurted, "wait till Kate sees you!"

"Peter, how nice!" Jonno's mother followed Alison into the kitchen and, while she was kissing Peter, Jonno looked at the muscles that swelled firmly above his friend's elbows. Peter's shoulders were broader and his legs sturdier. Even his wrists looked thicker. For the first time in his life, Jonno felt like the ninety-five-pound weakling in an ad for bodybuilding.

Peter grinned, which was normal, and blushed, which was not—whether because of his mother's kiss or Alison's comment, Jonno couldn't guess.

"Where is Kate, anyway?" Peter asked.

One of Peter's talents was knowing how to make everyone in the family feel important, Jonno thought. "Kate's sleeping, as usual," he told Peter.

"How could anyone sleep? This place sounds like Grand Central Station!" Kate grumbled her way down the stairs, in bare feet and green-sprigged white flannel nightgown, tumbling hair a dark cloud on her shoulders. Three steps from the bottom, she sat down abruptly, green eyes wide and cheeks flaming. "Peter? I wouldn't have come bombing down here like this if I'd known you were here."

So what was her problem all of a sudden? wondered Jonno. She'd been wandering around in granny gowns for years in front of his friends, without anyone ever taking notice. But here was Peter staring back at her, his face nearly as red as hers; and in this roomful of usually noisy people there was another beat of silence.

"Kate, how's it goin'?" Peter managed finally.

"Fine." Kate's green eyes seemed to say more, but she only hugged her knees and added, "So what are you guys up to anyway?"

"Biking to Mooncusser Beach," said Jonno.

"Want to come?" asked Peter. Carrying niceness much too far, Jonno thought. Just what was going on here?

"Sure." Kate jumped to her feet. "If I can have five minutes for a shower."

What was going on here? Jonno had never known Kate to ride a bike more than five miles voluntarily.

"Kate," said Jonno's mother quickly. "Today's a perfect day to look for that bathing suit you need so badly."

"Oh, that's right." Kate looked really disappointed. "Well, Peter, maybe I'll see you when you get back."

She was acting stranger than usual, Jonno thought; and Phil and Jessica Ayres exchanged one of their quizzical looks.

"Don't let us keep you, guys," his father said.

"Do be careful," said his mother and grandmother, like a Gilbert and Sullivan chorus.

34

"Am I glad to get out of there," breathed Jonno as they swung onto their bikes.

Peter grinned sympathetically, but on the verge of the lane he braked, wiggling his eyebrows like a bad imitation of Groucho Marx. "I dunno, Jonno. If I had your sister Kate to look at, I might not leave at all." Jonno struggled to control a disbelieving glare, and Peter added lamely, "Your family's pretty cool."

What had become of the days when he freely told Peter he was crazy? Jonno was suddenly shy about contradicting this impressive new Peter. He decided to concentrate on getting his five-speeder up the hill to the main road at the same pace as Peter's twelve.

From the top of the rise ahead, a mile of gentle, downhill coasting stretched toward town. "Peter," Jonno hollered, "let's stop at the general store so I can fill my tires."

Bending over his rear tire with the air hose seemed a likely time for making a question casual. "Say, Peter," Jonno said, staring at the pressure gauge and remembering fog and shadow, "you haven't heard anything odd on the outer beach, have you? I was there with Pip yesterday when the fog was coming in, and we thought we heard some really weird music."

Peter stood with his hands on his hips and every muscle showing, giving unreasonable attention to every passing car. "Unhh," he grunted noncommittally.

"Have you heard anything like that out there?" Jonno persisted. If Peter was going to be so blasé, Jonno wasn't about to tell him that the sound was scary.

In the absence of even an answering grunt, Jonno straightened and glanced over his shoulder. Peter was staring after a disappearing station wagon, and the two giggling girls on the tailgate were staring back at Peter. Jonno could feel his jaw setting. The family bustle had made talking impossible back at Gram's; the need for riding single file made it hard to talk on the bikes; and now that they were in a spot where they could communicate, Peter was standing around looking like Superman.

"Peter!" Jonno exploded. "I'm asking you something and all you do is stare at traffic." Good grief, he sounded like a caricature of Doug's father. "What are you doing, anyway?"

Peter whirled toward him with the old winning grin. "Whoa, Jonno!" He threw his arms out with a thumbs-up gesture. "I'm scopin'!"

"You're what?"

"Scopin'! Great sport—I'll tell you next year how it compares with football." Jonno was getting madder by the syllable. "Jonno—scopin': short for S-C-O-P-I-N-G. Latest code for the ancient art of girl-watchin'."

It sounded so dumb that Jonno didn't know what to say. It was really depressing to find old up-and-at-'em Peter smitten with standing around staring at traffic. Well, at girls in traffic. Girls! His own life had too many of them already.

Peter now gave him exaggerated, full attention, eyes rounded and eyebrows raised. "So what 'something' were you askin' me?" As if he were talking to a first-grader. Even Jonno's father had stopped talking to him that way long ago.

Jonno shrugged. "Nothing much. I heard some strange music on the beach yesterday, is all."

"Over on the spit? I haven't been there much this year," Peter said as Jonno nodded. "Scopin's better at the public beach."

Jonno swallowed a groan and got back on his bike. The clouds were lowering. If Peter scoped his way through the village, they might be drenched before they even reached the bike trail.

But by the time the village was behind them, Jonno realized that scoping gave him one advantage. Peter's pace was so leisurely that the difference between the bikes was no problem. Even on the safe, wide trail through the bayside marshes, there were other bikers and hikers, some of them female. So Peter, who used to race everywhere, had little interest in hurrying.

Only when they had crossed the highway to the National Seashore headquarters and struck off on the trail that led through pine woods to the beach did Peter sound like his old self. "Hey, Jonno," he called, pedaling down the first hill, "I'll race you to the Coast Guard station!"

It was a fairly hair-raising trail for fast riding, lined with signs advising caution, and Jonno had to work hard to keep up. Laughing at Peter's hoots and hollers didn't help either. By the time they labored up the last steep hill to the Coast Guard station, Jonno's thigh muscles throbbed and his breath burned in his throat, but he felt good inside. The last three miles were like all the other summers he remembered: good times and good tiredness.

He'd be glad to transfer lunch from the backpack to his stomach. "Let's eat on the bench here," he called as he followed Peter into the hilltop parking lot. Behind, but not by much. "I think you won," he added, swinging off the bike.

"All those muscles give you an unfair advantage."

Peter tried to look modest, but accepted a fat ham sandwich as if it were a trophy.

"How did you grow so much so fast, anyway?" asked Jonno.

"I've been using weights and stuff, for football," Peter said. "But partly it just happened. You just change as you get older."

Jonno munched on his sandwich and stared down across Mooncusser Beach toward the inlet. It was pretty scary to think he might just get his life under control sometime, only to change in a couple of seasons into an almost different person. If that lay ahead, he wouldn't think about it. He'd wrap himself in the rituals of all their other summers, and hope that time would let him be.

Revived by the food, he stood up and stretched. Down the beach was a landmark, a venerable shack where a long-ago naturalist had spent a blustery year and written a famous diary. A little, leaning, weather-beaten place, with a plaque that told you you'd been somewhere special. "Want a look at the Outermost House before we start back?" he asked Peter.

"Nah. I mean, it's gone." Peter stretched an arm lazily toward the Eastmoor Inlet. "See how wide the inlet looks, how much of this beach is gone? That big storm last winter washed over the beach here. It carried a lot of dunes into the marsh, and Outermost House went with them."

"No!" Jonno's eyes stung surprisingly. The old weathered shack was one of his touchstones, a place that beckoned like home plate, or the home base in a game of Fifty Scatter.

Peter eyed him curiously. "I know it's gone, Jonno. They found the plaque in the marsh after the storm, and my grandmother sent us a newspaper picture of it. If you don't believe me, run down and see for yourself."

He needed to run somewhere. "You comin'?"

"Nah." Peter laid his poncho on the brow of the hill overlooking the beach. "I've run enough for one day."

Down the slope toward the beach Jonno ran, and on along the marsh to a dead cedar tree that was their mark for turning seaward to the house. His breath was rasping again as he turned away from the marsh and along the dunes' lee. Not far from here the shack should be, but except for the tree his landmarks were gone. The moonscape of flattened dunes running to the marsh was convincing evidence that Peter was right. The Outermost House and its sheltering sandhills had vanished.

Jonno turned and trudged back toward the hill crowned with the white clapboard Coast Guard station. He expected to find Peter asleep, but found him propped against a tree surveying the tourists who had come to see the view.

"Scopin'?" Jonno turned back to look down the ravaged beach.

"Sure." Peter grinned up at him. "You'll get the hang of it. I've got a buddy who's threatening to write a book. *Wilson's Guide to Ultimate Scopin'*, with chapters like 'Subtle Scopin': Disguises for the Scoper,' subsection 'Sunglasses,' and 'Rating the Scopee, One-to-Ten System Preferred.' I'm just helpin' with the research."

"Huh." Jonno made a noise he hoped was more noncommittal than insulting.

"Speaking of girls," Peter went on, "your sister, by the way, is a definite eight-goin'-on-nine. We are talkin' World-Class Cute."

Jonno searched for the kindest thing he could honestly say about Kate. "Well," he told Peter, "you caught her at a good time. She looks pretty good in the morning before she starts working on herself."

Peter gave him another look designed for a dense first-grader. "So was I right? About the house?"

"It sure is gone. The dunes too."

"And my grandfather says the rest of the beach is going. Some summer soon there just won't be a Mooncusser Beach." Peter smiled about that, too.

"Doesn't that bother you at all?" demanded Jonno.

Peter shrugged. "Everything changes. Ya gotta go with the flow."

I'm tired, Jonno thought, as the first drops of rain began to fall. It was going to be a long ride home.

"Haarrhhh! Haarrhhh! Haarrhhh!"

Jonno's crowd sounds echoed the waves rolling in to shore.

"It's the last of the ninth, sports fans; the score is tied at two apiece, and the spectators here are on their feet. They want to know if the Sox can pull this one out of the fire, and here comes Rice to see what his big bat can do. *Haarrhhh!"*

A gull riding the southwest wind cast a shadow over Jonno's dice. He had never brought the baseball game to the beach before, and after two days of rain he had had his fill of games from Bingo to Twenty Questions. But right now it was too cool to swim, and he had promised not to "wander off," as Gram put it, before the rest of the family got there. So he'd finish the game he had called last night on account of yawning.

At least today had dawned cloudless, and the goose on Gram's weather vane was facing seaward, which usually meant fair weather. All that remained of the storm was the stiff breeze blowing the birds around, and all that remained of Jonno's last visit to this beach was his memory of cold hands and unearthly music. He had tried to return in the rain to find some sign that would tell him he had not imagined the whole encounter. He would have been reassured

41

to find either an earthly footprint or a specter walking the beach again. But for two days fog had lain on the bluff like a blanket, seeping even into Gram's lane, as forbidding as a sign saying DANGER: NO ADMITTANCE.

"Haarrhhh!"

Jonno sat cross-legged on a towel, facing the ocean and the sun, and zipped his sweatshirt a little higher as another gust scattered sand across the gameboard.

More sand spattered across his peaceful spot as Alison skidded past him on her way to test the water. Oh, crud, thought Jonno. Here comes the caravan.

Nothing could keep the Ayreses off the beach if the sun was shining. Though Jonno liked to slip down alone carrying only what he could roll in a beach towel, the rest of the family always arrived looking like a bunch of Bedouins prepared for a week's encampment. He could tell Kate was coming because he could already hear the radio. "OOOOOoo. oooOOO. OOOooo."

"Ugh, ugh, ugh," Jonno muttered to himself. He looked over his shoulder. Hampers, beach chairs, practically suitcases, as usual. "Don't mind that commotion in the stands, sports fans—that's Kate Ayres, the well-known rock freak, who as we all know never makes a move without her private band and amplifiers! Why, Miss Ayres," he added as Kate plodded up and dropped everything but her radio, "I have to say we are stunned to see you here at the ballpark so early in the day."

"Don't start with me, Jonno!" Kate snapped, and then seemed to make an unusual effort to restrain herself. "I refuse to let you make me mad. Since Alison woke me up to see the sun, I intend to enjoy it." She set down her radio, twisted her outstretched arms in front of her, and shuddered. "Have you ever seen such a wimpy tan? Next to Peter I look like a corpse."

Jonno sighed. What she really looked like next to Peter was a new convert to a cult. Kate was as tan as anyone in the family, and whatever shade she was seemed fine with Peter, who had spent last night in Gram's living room letting Kate beat him in five out of six games of checkers.

As their parents unfolded chairs, Alison scampered up the slope from the icy water and sent another shower of sand across Jonno's lap. He let his chin sink to his chest and closed his eyes.

"*Haarrhhh!* We've talked before about this unpredictable New England weather, but this may be a first, sports fans. This game is being called again, on account of sandstorms!"

Jonno stuffed his score sheets inside the battered cardboard box, slipped on its rubber bands, and scrambled to his feet. "I'm going to jog down to the public beach, okay? I'll be back by lunchtime."

Interest flickered in Kate's eyes, and for a moment Jonno was afraid she was going to join him. But she went back to her suntan lotion, with a pointed "If you see anyone I know, be sure to say 'hello.'"

It was Alison who jumped up and down, spoiling his escape. "Oh, Jonno, can I go, too? Mom, Dad, can I?"

"It's all right with me if it's okay with Jonathan."

It wasn't okay. He'd be heading beyond the place where the shadow had vanished in the fog, and he really wanted to go alone, to scour the beach for any trace that could affirm his sanity. But he didn't want to stand around and

43

argue, so he nodded and set off at a slow trot toward the cluster of sea-washed rocks that lay halfway to the public beach.

The storm had swept the beach of tracks and sand-castles and left its own souvenirs—bits of driftwood, lots of seaweed. The blare of Kate's radio faded, and for a while there were only sea sounds, the clicking of his ankle, and the huffing and puffing of Alison behind him. Then he began to be aware of a hum that wavered yet grew more distinct as he ran farther. He had gone another twenty-five yards before he knew it was the music again, the music he had heard in the fog three days before.

Like an animal catching a scent he froze, staring down the beach. No doubt, it was the music. In today's bright, clear air, it sounded more cheerful, a tune that climbed through the morning like a salute to the sun.

Alison caught up with him in a flurry of jellylike arms and legs, pretending to be done in. Or maybe not pretending. "Boy, Jonno, am I glad you finally decided to rest! Am I ever pooped! Do I ever need a Coke! Or a milkshake and maybe some onion rings! Can we go to the Snack Shack?"

Jonno felt guilty about having made her run so far, but furious about the noisy chatter. It seemed that everything Al said ended with an exclamation point.

"Darn it, Al—can't you be quiet, even for a minute?" Fists clenched with the effort to hear and understand, he shook himself a little and tried to calm down. No menace today, but still a mystery. "I'm trying to hear something."

For once Alison was still. Her blue eyes grew rounder as she listened, too. "What is that? A parade?"

"I don't know," said Jonno, as calmly as he could. "I

44

think it's somewhere near where we're going, so we can just walk fast. You don't have to run."

He needed a little time to think. This was his mystery, and he wanted to solve it alone. But here was Alison, all wide eyes, quick ears, and big mouth, and if he made a big thing of trying to divert her or send her back, she'd be more curious than ever. Not to mention mad as a wet hen. He sometimes trusted her with things he'd never tell Kate, but he wasn't ready to talk to anyone about those shivery minutes on the dune. So what he must do was pretend the sound was as new to him as it was to her. Not a word about the shadow in the fog. Most of all, not a word about how the music drew him.

With the rocks behind them and beach umbrellas sprouting on the sand ahead, the sound pealed on more clearly. Still they seemed not to gain on it but only to keep pace, as if the player were moving off toward the Snack Shack perched behind the dunes at the edge of the parking lot.

By the time they reached the boardwalk leading to the shack, they were almost running again. Jonno didn't want to lose his quarry now.

Jogging toward them was a lifeguard in an unmistakable electric-orange bathing suit.

"Excuse me," Jonno said to the brawny young man who nearly fell over him, "but do you know what that music is?"

"Oh, sure—it's a bagpipe," the guard said hurriedly. "Don't care for it much, myself. Look, I'm sorry to rush off, but I'm on duty." And he was gone.

Jonno had opened his mouth to ask more questions.

Disappointment turned to worry as he turned and realized that Alison had disappeared. And the music was getting louder again, as if the player—the piper?—were returning from the far end of the parking lot. Where in the world was Alison? In the rest room, or hanging around reading the menu at the shack; it always took her long enough to decide what she wanted. Well, she knew her way around here pretty well. Right now he had to see that bagpipe.

Jonno wiggled through the stream of beachgoers like a minnow trying to move against the tide. How could all these people turn their backs on the amazing sound in the parking lot?

Just ahead, at the Snack Shack, the tide was more like a whirlpool. And on the fringe of the bustle, leaning back with one foot braced against a post, was Peter, looking as if he were scanning the crowd for an expected friend. Jonno knew better, and hoped that being male he would escape notice.

"Heyyy, Jonno! How's it goin'?"

"Hi, Peter." He didn't want to stop now. "Have you seen Alison?"

"No, can't say I have, but she's a little short to be picked up in my normal scope. Is Kate here?"

"Up the beach," said Jonno shortly. "I'd better find Al."

"Hey!" said Peter, tossing his head toward the parking lot. "Is that your weird music?"

"Yah, yah, I think so. Want to come see?"

"Nah." Peter dismissed him with a wave. "The view is better here."

Jonno turned and dashed out onto the pavement of the parking lot. The macadam was warm, and here in the sunny lee of the dunes the swelling music sounded gloriously happy. One bagpipe? It sounded more like a whole men's chorus with the bass notes singing below the soaring, climbing tenors. Closer and louder.

There! Around a line of parked cars came a figure carrying an ungainly bundle of tubes and pouches. It was a tall man, broad-shouldered but spare, and a stiffness about the way he moved made Jonno certain he had been the shadow in the fog. He wore khaki shorts and sandals and a rumpled-looking shirt made of dull plaid, with the sleeves rolled up to his elbows. The clothes hung on his lean frame as if they had been with him for a long time, but they were much too normal to be ghostly.

This time at least Jonno could be sure that he was not imagining the figure and the wild music, for he could see as the piper came on that he was not alone. Behind him marched a ragtag retinue—two parking attendants in suntan uniforms and white caps, a jaunty beachgoer in a palm-tree-covered bathing suit and a straw porkpie hat. A fat little boy with a sandpail. And, oh no, that was where Alison Ayres had gone, for there she was bringing up the rear, grinning like a Cheshire cat!

The music stopped abruptly and another strain began, proud and compelling, a triumphant melody that Jonno had heard somewhere before—maybe in the movie that had lurked on the fringes of his memory the other day on the foggy beach. It was too much for Alison. She broke into her finest dancing-recital strut, and the man with the palm trees quickly called to the parking attendants to copy her step, so that the whole motley line high-stepped toward Jonno like part of a mad dress parade. Jonno was

47

mortified. He could hardly believe his sister's total hamminess. It was lucky Peter had stayed at the Snack Shack, so that Jonno could just pretend he didn't know her.

The piper seemed curiously unaware of the flurry of enthusiasm behind him, unmoved even by his own infectious music. He blew steadily into a pipe attached to a large leathery bag tucked under his left arm, and the muscles in his lean brown forearms rippled as his fingers flew along another pipe that hung below. He held himself straighter than anyone Jonno had ever seen, so that even as he moved he had the air of a figure carved in wood.

Jonno had a fleeting impression of shaggy, graying hair. Sun-weathered skin. Eyes the color of the sky before a northeaster. Keen and wary, those eyes met Jonno's for an instant, in a glance that sent a shiver down his backbone even in the sunshine. They were the most alive eyes Jonno had ever seen, and the most wistful—a boy's eyes caught in a lined, weathered face.

Now the plump little kid was banging out the rhythm on his sandpail, and Alison was going by with a big, stagy wave. He'd lose himself in the crowd by the shack until her embarrassing performance was over, Jonno decided. He began to move away before he turned to see where he was going, and found his nose buried in the chest of another lifeguard. Good grief, what would the guard think of him: a klutz with a crazy sister!

"Gosh," said Jonno, "I'm really sorry."

"No problem." The guard grinned down at him. "You might say my job is running into people. Anyway, that music's enough to make anybody a little excited, huh?"

Jonno couldn't say how glad he was to hear that someone as cool as a lifeguard thought the bagpipe was exciting.

"Fellow's been around quite a while this summer," the guard went on. "Visiting someone on the bluff, a buddy from some war or other. He's a real Scot, someone told me. Anyway, he sure can play those pipes!"

"Say!" As the music receded toward the parking lot entrance, the guard suddenly brushed past Jonno and picked up a soft, lumpy object lying where the piper had passed. "He must have dropped this. Looks like a tobacco pouch. Maybe you'd like to get it back to him."

So Jonno stood in the sun holding a pungent-smelling, mouse-colored leather bag, tied with a leather thong. It looked about a thousand years old, he thought. And he could just run it over to the piper, and this would all be over.

What would all be over?

The mystery of the piper and his music had begun to seem the most promising part of this vacation. But he wasn't going to chase after that stern-looking Scot. Not in front of all these people. Especially not in front of Alison Ayres. Especially not when Peter Baldwin might even now be "scopin'" the parking lot.

Jonno tucked the pouch into the pocket of his jeans, and patted the pocket for safekeeping. He'd return the pouch, but he'd find another time.

"I can tell you just where he's staying. In Colonel Farnum's attic! Grace Goodspeed says he's been there for weeks, a regular Man Who Came to Dinner."

Thus Gram solved the problem of finding the piper that night at supper. Alison was full of her performance in the parking lot, and Gram was full of typically pithy opinions.

"I understand they fought together in France during World War II, and of course Colonel Farnum was quite a hero, but this bagpipe player has raised a few eyebrows around here, I can tell you, what with the noise he makes and all that shrubbery." Gram added a neat dab of mustard to her corned beef. "And none too pleasant, from what I hear. He barely spoke to Grace Goodspeed when the Farnums introduced them."

"What shrubbery?" asked Jonno.

"And what's a Man Who Came to Dinner?" added Alison.

"Well, perhaps the Farnums have neatened him up a bit," said Gram, "but he arrived with a full beard and a wild head of hair that made him look like an overage rock star." Gram looked at Alison. "And, young lady, *The Man Who Came to Dinner* was a play only I remember, about a guest who wouldn't leave and ended up taking over the whole household."

"How old is he?" asked Kate. "And what does a bagpipe sound like, anyway?"

"Like a St. Patrick's Day parade," said Phil Ayres.

"Like a cat on the back fence at midnight!" said Gram.

Jessica Ayres laughed. "Oh, more musical than that, I think—maybe like an oboe with a sinus condition."

"I thought," said Alison, "that it sounded like the circus."

"Like a voice crying on the wind," Jonno blurted without thinking.

He knew he had said too much when his parents glanced at each other quickly and then stared at him with frank curiosity.

"Jonno, that's as close as you've come to poetry since we read Robert Frost when you were five, and you found me a birch tree that looked like a girl with her hair tossed down to dry," his father said.

How could he retreat now to pretending disinterest? For once Kate saved him, by repeating her question. "How old is he?"

"He must be sixty, though he doesn't act his age, or look it. Anyway, he's old enough to know better," Gram declared firmly.

"Better than what?" Alison's question seemed logical to Jonno, but Gram only raised her eyebrows.

So that was how Jonno came to be scuffing up the lane in the mist of morning. He had told the family he was walking to the general store. Unknowingly, Gram had told him where to deliver the tobacco pouch that was still tucked in his jeans' pocket, but the other things she'd reported about the piper had made Jonno pretty nervous about going to the Farnums' sprawling cottage with its weathered shingles and wide porches. Since he knew the Farnums only by sight, there'd be no cheery reunion to put him at his ease.

Now he wondered why he hadn't scurried after the piper yesterday. Then, he could have handed him the pouch without a word. Then, he could even have gotten Alison to give it to him. Then he wouldn't have had to worry about what to say to a man considered hostile by the most talkative lady Gram knew.

Jonno happened to know that Mrs. Goodspeed didn't mind quietness, because he'd hardly ever said a word to her and she always complimented his parents on his good manners. Dad said Mrs. Goodspeed was the only person he knew who didn't even notice if you never tried to get a word in edgewise. So if she thought the piper was cross and silent, how cross and silent could he seem to a kid who had kept his tobacco pouch a day too long?

Colonel Farnum's house rambled across a grassy knoll, separated only by bayberry thickets from cliff and inlet, dunes and sea. By the time Jonno stood on the long, low front porch, he was sure he should have done things differently. He could leave the pouch on the porch and run, but that would be risky with all the rabbits and raccoons that scavenged here. So he took a deep breath and knocked very gently on the weathered brown door. His throat felt tight and his hands were cold again. He waited, but no one came. He knocked again, hard enough to make his knuckles tingle, but though he could hear metallic rattlings inside as if breakfast were brewing, nothing happened at the door.

So he would have to try the massive brass knocker shaped like an anchor, and probably make a noise that would startle every bird and rabbit for a hundred yards around. The metal struck the wood like a gunshot in the still morning air, and this time Jonno heard light footsteps beyond the door.

It was opened by a slender, gray-haired woman wearing blue jeans and a long butcher's apron, who smiled as she discovered Jonno. "Good morning," she said cheerfully. "What can I do for you?"

"I'm sorry to bother you," said Jonno, wishing his voice sounded less squeaky, "but I think I found something that belongs to the man who plays the bagpipes, and I heard he was staying here."

He dug in his pocket for the velvety leather bag, as the lady looked first quizzical and then uncertain. As he held out the tobacco pouch, she looked over her shoulder as if she wondered whether to call someone else to the door.

"I'm Mrs. Farnum," she said finally, "and I'll be glad to give it to Mr. Loud. He's not feeling very well this morning, but he mentioned missing the pouch last night, and I know he'll be grateful you brought it back."

Mr. Loud. An appropriate name, Gram would say. "A cat howling on the back fence." That was Jonno's first thought.

His second was that all his tensed-up muscles were turning to mush with relief at not having to decide what to say to the piper. And then he realized that he had just surrendered to Mrs. Farnum his only connection with the shadow in the fog. His adventure was a big fizzle. He felt bitterly disappointed.

Mrs. Farnum looked puzzled. She probably wondered why he was still standing on her porch. "Thank you for coming," she said, and started to close the door.

"That's okay." Hopelessness gave Jonno a sudden burst of bravery. "But could you tell him, please, that I like his music?"

The door clicked shut, and Jonno turned and looked off across the vastness of the sea. That was that, he thought. Now I'd better run to the store before everyone at home starts asking questions.

"Hey, lad."

He was halfway down the path when the quiet voice startled him, for the breeze and birdcalls had hidden the sound of the door reopening.

Jonno spun around and found that the piper stood in the doorway, his left shoulder braced against the doorjamb, his right arm holding the screen door open. He gave Jonno a sort of salute with the pouch which he held in his right hand.

"I thank you for this. It's kind of a treasure."

It was soft and deep, the piper's voice. And he said his *r*'s as if his tongue got tangled in them.

Jonno moved back toward the house so that he could see into the porch shadows. "One of the guards found it yesterday, Mr. Loud, and he asked me to return it," he explained.

This morning the man looked more tired than fierce, as if he were holding himself together with great concentration. His eyes were red, and his jaw shadowy with unshaved beard. "Ah, well—I thank you both then," he said. And then, "I hear you like my music."

Jonno felt the man's gaze had grown keener suddenly, as if how he answered was important.

"Yah." Jonno ducked his head and nodded. "I do." Then he looked up again to the gray eyes, so direct that they demanded truth. He was surprised and dismayed to find himself elaborating. "Actually, it scared me a little at first."

"In the parking lot?" No wonder the man sounded baffled.

"Er—another time, on the beach in the fog."

"Aha. Well, some foe of the Scots once called the Black Watch Regiment 'the ladies from hell.' 'Ladies' was a reference to their kilts, but 'hell' was for their manners and their music. So ye're not the first, y'see, to find pipe music fearsome."

The man shifted his weight against the doorjamb. Jonno felt it was time to leave, but the piper's eyes held him.

"What's your name, lad?"

"Jonathan Ayres. They call me Jonno. Everybody but my mother. Anyway, I'm changing it to John when I get older."

Was there a twinkle in the cool gray eyes?

"Well, there's more to mine than 'Mr. Loud.' They call me Rob. And I'll not be down today, but we're on the beach a lot, me and the pipes. If you've ever a mind to walk with us, you're welcome."

Another salute with the pouch, and the big door closed again. He was gone.

Jonno sighed. For some crazy reason, he liked the idea

of sharing his beach with Mr. Loud and his bagpipes. But twice now, in less than a day, those pipes had thrown him off his guard. If his mouth was going to be as unpredictable as his throwing arm, he could be headed for trouble.

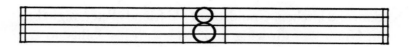

Jonno had caught the wave just right as it came across the sandbar. This must be how a bird feels on the wind, he thought, as he was lifted, launched, and sailed into the shallows.

"Whoo! Man, that baby was like an express train!" As the wave receded, Peter surfaced nearby, tossing water from his head and shoulders.

"It was great," Jonno gargled. He was still trying to spit out seawater the way Peter did, by squeezing it through his teeth. "A little better than the art show on the Green!"

With much rippling of enviable muscles, Peter hauled himself to his feet and raced back to meet the next big wave, but Jonno swallowed, letting the spent waves nudge him to and fro, thinking how glad he was not to be on the way to the village. This had been their first perfect beach day. Delicious and crystal-clear, with warm air lying on the sand as gently as a down-filled quilt, but warning that the town would be too hot for comfort.

Gram had hustled the rest of the family away to view a friend's woodcuts. Kate had gone along because the print-maker had once been her drawing teacher, Alison because she was told she was going. Jonno suspected he had escaped because of Gram's reluctance to include Peter, who had spent a remarkable lot of time lately in her living room and kitchen. Grandson of old friends Peter might be, but Gram was growing impatient with his ability to eat absentmindedly while doing anything else at all. Jonno had heard enough mutterings about army ants and locust plagues in the past few days to suppose he owed his reprieve to Peter.

"Hey, Jonno! The waves are really comin' up!" Peter was washed in again, whooping. He dragged himself erect and spat glorious twin fountains. "You gotta get your butt in gear and catch these big ones!" Wet or dry, Peter was never one to lie around thinking.

Jonno was on his feet, two steps toward the sandbar, when he realized that he heard the bagpipe. Cupping his hands for an eyeshade, he stopped in the shallows and scrutinized the upper beach. That had to be Rob Loud. A stirring in each patch of sunners marked his passing.

It was Jonno's first sight of the piper since their meeting on the Farnums' porch. This once, the timing was ideal. He was alone—except for Peter. He'd have to tell Peter something.

"Yo, Peter!" he hollered after the muscular, receding back, and Peter half-turned, looking quizzical. "I'm goin' to see Mr. Loud—the piper."

Peter rejoined him in a lunging run. "You're kiddin'! The waves are perfect!"

Jonno didn't argue. He turned and waded out of the water. "Why don't you come along?" he called over his shoulder. He was gambling on Peter's liking company, but he himself was going anyway.

On the way up the beach slope, he snatched his T-shirt and slung his tied-together moccasins around his neck.

Rob Loud was some fifty yards beyond him, striding strongly if a bit lopsidedly, and playing steadily. Jonno broke into a jog and was not surprised when Peter loped up beside him.

"Hey, Jonno, are you losin' your cool?" Peter slowed his long stride to Jonno's. "Why am I doin' this?"

Jonno chuckled to himself. Now Peter sounded like Doug's father.

To Peter he threw a confiding look. "He seems like a nice guy. I found something of his, and he talked to me the other day when I took it to the Farnums'."

Peter frowned. "How do you know he'll want you along?"

"He invited me."

"Well," Peter grumbled, rocking his head side to side as they drew abreast of the piper, "I didn't get a personal invitation."

Mr. Loud's gray glance swept toward them, old and young and bright. Jonno waved and was rewarded with a wink and a beckoning jerk of the gray head. But the piper went on striding toward the inlet.

"What are we gonna do?" hissed Peter. "March all the way to the inlet, like part of a parade?"

Jonno grinned. "Think of it, Peter—you can scope the whole beach! I'm just gonna walk along and look for shells and listen to the music."

Peter was momentarily distracted by a lithe blond jogger in a red tank suit, but he still grumbled. "It's sure not your basic Top Forty!"

Whatever the piper was playing, it did go on and on. It was the longest piece Jonno had ever heard that wasn't

Beethoven. And sad. When at last it ended, Mr. Loud swung the pipes to the crook of his arm and stopped walking.

"So, Jonno, you found me. And who's this?"

"Mr. Loud," said Jonno, "this is Peter Baldwin."

The piper nodded. "Glad to know you, Peter Baldwin. How was your swim? And are you a fan of Highland music, too, then?"

"The waves were great, sir," said Peter with a sidelong glare at Jonno. "And your music is . . . very unusual."

"Mr. Loud," Jonno interjected quickly, "what was that you were just playing?"

The man started up the beach again, his steps a bit more halting than before. "That was 'Squintin' Patrick's Flames of Wrath.' A slice of Highland history. Part of the classical music for the pipes, the *pibroch*."

"Pee brook" sounded like the funniest name yet for a piece of music, and Peter hooted predictably.

With subtle tightening of jaw and eyelids, Mr. Loud's face hardened as he turned to Peter. "That's a Gaelic word." His voice was still quiet.

"And who," asked Jonno quickly, "was Squinting Patrick?"

"Ah. A grievin' chieftain who burned his enemies' chapel, with their whole clan inside, in revenge for the massacre of his own family. Those Highlanders, they didn't fool around, y'know."

Jonno didn't know, and Peter looked startled, too. But Mr. Loud matter-of-factly readjusted his pipes and began another tune.

"Hsst! Jonno!" Peter stopped and looked back toward

his favorite sandbar. "I got a major kick out of 'pee brook,' but this stuff is really freaky. Besides which, he talks like a history teacher."

Sometimes Peter's muscles were more impressive than his imagination. "Doesn't it make you curious?" said Jonno.

"Not curious enough to miss those waves," said Peter. "And there's not a girl in range for scopin'. I'm headin' back." He started off and paused, clearly expecting Jonno to go along.

Instead, Jonno gazed for a long moment at the sea. He was conscious of Peter poised on his right, and Mr. Loud pacing away on his left. Already the sun cast their shadows long toward the water. There'd be other waves, but probably not another piper.

"So long, Peter," he said, and turned to follow Rob Loud.

Within a few steps he was enveloped in the sound of pipes. It was like that last good wave he'd ridden, lifting and carrying him, compelling. For the first time ever he felt a part of music.

On Mr. Loud went, from shorter tune to shorter tune. He played some music that felt like a parade, some that seemed a dance, and the melody that had sounded so gloomy in the fog, but now became a lullaby. They had gone a mile or more, to the place where the beach ended and the tide raced through the inlet, when the pipes pealed out the rousing march from the parking lot.

"What was that?" Jonno hurled into the momentary pause at the song's finish, and Rob Loud turned from the blowpipe with a sidelong glance of surprise.

"'Scotland the Brave'? I thought even all you Yanks knew that one!"

"And all those faster ones?"

"Marches, some. Strathspeys and reels, for Highland dancing." For the first time in half an hour, the piper looked all around him. "We lost yer mate, then?"

"He had an appointment," Jonno lied diplomatically.

The corners of Mr. Loud's mouth twitched. "But ye're not bored yet?"

Jonno shook his head.

"Which piece was best?"

"Maybe the slow one, before 'Scotland the Brave.' The one that sounded like a lullaby."

The piper nodded as if he were pleased. "'Skye Boat Song,' that was. Ye're half-right—it's a sort of lullaby, but a war song as well." And to Jonno's surprise, the man swung down his pipes again, threw his head back, and began to sing in a sure bass, gravelly but true:

"Speed, bonnie boat, like a bird on the wing,
    'Onward,' the sailors cry!
    'Carry the lad that's born to be king
        Over the sea to Skye!'"

He kept time with his free arm as Jonno's mother sometimes did to urge her singers on, brandishing his clenched fist at a cruising sea gull.

"Loud the winds howl, loud the waves roar,
    Thunder clouds rend the air;
    Baffled our foes stand on the shore,
    Follow they will not dare."

Then he swung toward the harbor, craning his neck to follow a flight of terns:

"Though the waves leap, soft shall ye sleep,
    Ocean's a royal bed;
    Rock'd in the deep, Flora will keep
    Watch by your weary head."

The song was well named. The melody rose and fell like a boat rocked by the sea.

"Ahh, blast, the last verse escapes me!" Abruptly Mr. Loud turned his back to the inlet and hoisted the pipes to his shoulder again.

"But what's Skye?" Jonno asked quickly.

"An island off the coast of Scotland."

"And who's 'the lad that's born to be king'?"

"Ah," said Rob. "Bonnie Prince Charlie. A headstrong Scot who wanted the English crown. Flora MacDonald took him to her family's stronghold on Skye when the English had wiped out his army. But c'mon, Jonathan Ayres, enough of this spracklin'. This ramblin'," he added, seeing Jonno's puzzled look. "We'd best head back while my leg's still fit."

Through another mile and more of music, Jonno walked, ran, and skipped stones. He half expected to grow tired of all this and start yearning for a good game of catch. But he was swept on by the music, back to the place where they'd begun.

After a triumphant tune that Jonno liked as much as anything he'd heard before, Rob Loud swung down the pipes with a final sort of flair, and flexed his fingers.

"What—" Jonno began.

"'All the Bluebonnets Are Over the Border.' About Charlie's fighters and their caps." Like his eyes, his smile was young. "You like that one?"

With a lump in his throat from the music, Jonno only nodded. The man's eyes darkened and a stillness came over him, sudden as the smile.

"Aye. There was a day I thought I'd never want to play it again, but I like it, too." He seemed to shake off a shadow as he turned back to Jonno. "Have ye liked music always, Jonno?"

Jonno looked into the cloudy gray eyes and swallowed all his tactful evasions. "No," he said. "I never knew I did, till now."

Rob Loud gave him a searching look, but only said, as he trudged toward the dunes, "That's a glad thing to discover." He settled himself against the low shoulder of the first rise he came to, and stretched his right leg out carefully. "What I've discovered is that I can't play those pipes as long as once I could." He sighed as he let his head fall back onto a pillow of cooling sand, and then he closed his eyes.

No more words came. The special quiet of the beach in late afternoon settled over them, and Jonno began to fear that the conversation was over. It even seemed that Mr. Loud was going to take a nap, which would certainly have infuriated Grace Goodspeed and didn't please him very much either. The difference was that Mrs. Goodspeed surely would have known how to keep Mr. Loud awake.

Jonno clambered a little farther up the dune and wriggled himself into a comfortable hollow with his arms wrapped around his knees. "Is it hard? Playing the pipes?" he asked as loudly as seemed reasonable.

"Um," murmured Rob Loud sleepily. "Well, I've been at it so long I hardly think about it, but it takes a fair amount of lung power. And some years before you get it to sound the way you'd like."

"It sounds amazing," said Jonno. As they had at the Farnums', his words tumbled out less carefully than usual. "When I heard you the first time, from up on the bluff, I wasn't even sure that it was music. I mean," he went on, wary of sounding tactless, "there's lots of music at our house—my father knows jazz, and my sister plays rock, and my mother loves classical, but the bagpipe is . . ." He searched for the word and couldn't find it, though he felt somehow a piper would know what he was trying to say.

Rob Loud opened his eyes and cocked an eyebrow at Jonno. "Unique?"

That was it. One-of-a-kind special. Jonno nodded.

"Aye," the man replied, "though growin' up in a wee village on a shingly shore, I'd little to compare it with. We hadn't the variety of noise to choose from that ye've got today." Mr. Loud raised himself on his elbows and stared at the sea. "But the pipes wouldn't have survived for two thousand years if they weren't special. It's a rare sound. Hard to describe." He cocked his head to one side as if to shake the right words loose. "Kind of elemental. 'Compar'd with these, Italian trills are tame.'"

Jonno blinked, and Rob Loud chuckled at his befuddlement. "That's from a bloke more skilled with words than me. Robert Burns, a poet and great champion of Scots' music, who made fun of more highfalutin tastes. I was named for him, by the way, Jonathan Ayres. You ought to know there's others of us blessed with romantic mothers. I think mine hoped I might turn out a poet."

"But you turned out a piper."

Jonno smiled, but another shadow crossed Rob Loud's face. "And a gypsy," he replied.

Jonno tried retreating to a safer subject. "Mr. Loud, I'm glad you're feeling better."

"Not 'Mister,' lad." The man looked at Jonno and his voice lightened. "I've knocked about, 'eternal swervin,' as Robbie Burns also said, 'nae rules nor road observin,' and there's hardly anyone's ever called me Mister." His voice was even burrier when he quoted Robert Burns. "'Sergeant,' and some things less complimentary—but not 'Mister.' At least, no one I liked. So you now, go back and try that line again, with 'Rob.'"

"Okay. Rob," said Jonno carefully, "I'm glad you're feeling better."

Rob managed to shrug with head and hands and shoulders, in a way both cheerful and resigned. "I've a leg that's in less than its former braw condition, dating from about the time I got to know John Farnum, and every now and then it gets the better of me. Then I'm inclined to a double ration of whiskey or a pint too many. And the next day I regret it."

Jonno's mind flew from his father's gallery of remembered characters to his grandmother's raised eyebrows. "You mean, you had a hangover?" There went his mouth again.

Rob grinned ruefully. "I did. As well as a sore leg. But I try to limit myself to one binge a fortnight," he said drily, watching Jonno's mouth close. "Enough of troubles. So you'd heard the pipes, then, before the other day in the parking lot? Here, or up the brae there?"

Judging from Rob's gesture, the brae meant the bluff, so Jonno nodded. "Both. I followed the sound to the beach, from a place up there that's amazing, too. At the top of the wooden stairs. Sometimes I go there just to look."

"I know it," said Rob quite seriously. "It reminds me of a spot on the side of Ben Cairn that I loved when I was growing up. It's unique, too, a place like that. Just like the sound of pipes."

Jonno hugged his knees tighter and decided to risk feeling foolish. "It makes me feel full of . . . peace, I guess, or hope," he said.

"Or maybe wild surmise," said Rob Loud.

That had a good ring to it. "But I'm not sure what that means," Jonno admitted.

"Ahh . . . a feeling you can guess how big the world is and you want to drink it all in. A sense of endless possibilities," Rob rumbled, staring off toward Portugal. "That's from a poem, too, that phrase, about 'stout Cortez when with eagle eyes/He star'd at the Pacific—and all his men/Look'd at each other with a wild surmise—/Silent, upon a peak in Darien.'"

Jonno was struck silent. From his fifth-grade list of Great Explorers, he happened to know it was Balboa who had found the Pacific Ocean in 1513, but for once the facts didn't seem as important to him as the feeling. "Wild surmise." That was just how he felt on the bluff, but he had never expected that this sinewy man who made such wild music would start spouting poetry like his father.

He felt Rob looking at him quizzically. "That sounds," said Jonno finally, "like something my father would quote me. He's an English teacher."

"Then he can quote you a lot more Keats than me," said Rob. "I was no great scholar, you understand. We had to memorize all sorts of stuff that bored me silly at the time. But it made more sense to me as I got older." He scooped up some sand and watched it sift through his fingers, as intent as a toddler with a sandpail.

"What was it like," Jonno asked, "growing up near the ocean?"

"A bit bleak, but glorious. I'd play the pipes along the strand, and whenever I wasn't at that or raisin' Cain, I was in the water."

Despite Rob's graying thatch of hair and weather-beaten face, it wasn't hard to imagine him as a laughing brown boy, hurling himself into waves. Something like Peter. No, different. Deeper.

"Was it just like swimming here?" Jonno asked.

"I can't really say, lad. I've not swum here, or anywhere, for a good long while. Not since the lot of us nearly drowned one day in France, trying to get from a landing boat to the beach. It never seemed like sport again."

The man was full of surprises. "But you must have been a good swimmer!" Jonno said incredulously.

"Aye. Only I lacked practice carryin' seventy-odd pounds of equipment and the pipes, with people on the beach shootin' at me," said Rob. "They had to leave us too far offshore, y'see, because of mines, and a lot of lads just drowned before they ever fired a shot."

People on the beach shooting. "Were you there on D-Day?" Jonno asked.

"Aye."

Jonno looked out across the utter peace of his beach and his side of the sea and didn't want to imagine it covered with blood and guns and struggling bodies. He realized, too, with a start, that most of the beach was now in shadow.

"Omigosh!" he exclaimed, unwinding and leaping to his feet in one spring. "I can't be late for supper."

"Don't fret yerself, lad—John Farnum's battered old beach buggy is tucked in a fold of the dunes back there. We'll spin by the general store for my pipe tobacco, and then I'll run you home."

Jonno struggled with his conscience. He had a lot more questions to ask. He had never known anyone old enough to be his grandfather who talked to him almost as if he were a grown-up, but seemed to remember just what it was like to be a kid. Jonno was absolutely sure that Rob remembered. So he didn't want the afternoon to end, but he was supposed to let his parents know whenever he took off in a new direction.

"What time is it, do you think, Mr. . . . Rob?" he asked.

Rob turned his head and squinted at the sinking sun. "Time for a drink, perhaps. Not quite time for supper. What d'ye say, lad?"

There was no harm in going, Jonno thought. They'd be home by the time he could get back to Gram's and ask permission. And how could he talk about dumb rules to a man so full of battle tales and wild surmise?

So Jonno stood up. "Sure, Rob," he said with more confidence than he really felt. "Let's go after your tobacco."

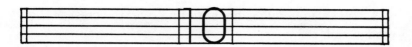

Colonel Farnum's dune buggy fit right into the spirit of the afternoon, thought Jonno. It was a converted jeep with the frayed and frazzled look of an old campaigner. The seat cushions in particular looked as if they had fallen victim to a few explosions.

"Never mind," Rob chuckled as Jonno stared at a protruding spring, "she's livelier than she looks, ol' Maudie. She'll get you home, sooner or later."

He could have taken that as a warning, Jonno thought later, but the ride began innocently enough. After a few ominous groans, the old engine hiccuped into motion, and Rob eased the jeep along the shifting ruts of the beach-buggy track with what seemed like extreme caution. At the junction with the main road, he paused carefully and turned to Jonno with a reassuring grin.

"Now she's crackin'," said Rob cheerfully, and without warning swung the jeep onto the far side of the road. Jonno was suddenly paralyzed with fear. If anything came over the rise ahead, they'd be bound for a head-on collision. He glanced at Rob in horror and found him relaxed at the wheel. He found himself pressing urgently back, away from the windshield, ready to duck or throw his arms in front of his face — and still no words would come.

A Volkswagen bug came barreling over the crest of the road ahead.

"Damn!" Rob clapped both lean hands onto the steering wheel and hauled it hard to the right. Behind Jonno's right ear a horn blared. Back there, in his proper lane, a teenager with a red Afro, driving a van laden with surfboards, was gesticulating wildly.

"It's the infernal turns that mess me up," Rob muttered, pulling the jeep back from the verge of the road. He made furious beckoning gestures at the fellow in the Afro, urging him to pass. "Come on then, ye noisy bugger—or else have pity on a poor pilgrim who's not used to drivin' on the wrong side of the road!"

Slowly Jonno began to unstick himself from the lumpy seat. Maybe this outing was a big mistake. What did Rob mean, "drivin' on the wrong side of the road"? He found Rob giving him an appraising gray look and wished he would keep his eyes on the road.

"Did ye not know," Rob went on calmly, his foot clamped on the accelerator as they churned round the next bend, "that in Great Britain we drive on the left side? I'm fine here, y'see, on a straightaway. But at intersections, especially comin' from a one-lane track like that back there, it gets confusin'."

With that Rob pulled toward the center of the road to pass a line of bikers, and swerved back beyond them to avoid a pickup truck coming in the other direction. Jonno had just opened his eyes and begun to relax again when a tan blur slid across his line of vision. Without a sideways glance, a little old lady in a vintage Ford had sailed into their lane from a driveway barely ahead.

"Damnation! Ye nitwit, numbskull, and nincom-*poop!*"
As Rob ground the brake into the jeep's floorboards,
Jonno grabbed the door again and braced his feet to keep
from flying forward.

Rob went on muttering in a private sort of way, and
Jonno quietly decided to hold on until they reached the
parking lot. This was certainly his most exciting trip ever
to the general store. A little like the Krazy Kars ride at
Portsmouth Park. If he'd expected it, he might have tried to
make excuses and missed all the excitement! Still, he
would be gladder than usual to see the general store.

Half a mile farther on, without a signal, the tan Ford
veered abruptly into the sandy parking lot Jonno had been
watching for.

"Good riddance!" cried Rob with a great rolling *r*.

"But, Rob," blurted Jonno hurriedly, "that's the turn you
want!"

"Right full rudder, then!" With no hesitation Rob pulled
hard right on the jeep's steering wheel, careened through
the opening clearly marked EXIT and jolted to a stop by the
porch of Mr. Cody's store.

As the sandy cloud kicked up by their rackety arrival
settled, Jonno realized that they had pulled up next to the
same tan Ford—and that the small lady glaring at them
from its driver's seat was none other than his grandmother's gossipy friend, Grace Goodspeed. She it was who'd
disapproved of Rob so noisily before. Surely she'd not
miss the chance to interrogate Gram about her grandson's
travels with "the overage hippie." So his family was bound
to find out that he had taken off with Rob without a word.
Jonno gauged his distance from the store's sagging cedar

door and from Mrs. Goodspeed, and concluded there was no escape.

It might have been all right if Mrs. Goodspeed had not bustled out of her little tan car with all her righteousness intact. Jonno was immensely relieved when she mounted Mr. Cody's porch with scarcely a glance in his direction. Then he discovered she had merely sought a proper pulpit for giving Rob a lecture.

"Has no one told you," she demanded, planting herself on the porch directly above the spot where Rob alighted from the jeep, "that in this progressive country there's a law against tailgating?"

That was when Rob's neck turned a dull red under his tan, but he spoke quietly enough. "Mistress Goodspeed!" The words rolled out like a judgment, softened by a slight inclining of his head that was like the beginning of a mocking bow. "Perhaps ye failed t' notice I was virtually on the edge of your driveway when you decided to depart it." His r's rumbled. "Perhaps I should point out you were fortunate not to have us in your backseat."

Mrs. Goodspeed snorted sanctimoniously. "You needn't try to change the subject, Mr. Loud. I get very tired of visitors who try to intimidate me into racing along with them. Not to mention, endangering the lives of our children! And"—she turned her searchlight gaze on Jonno—"if that's you, Jonathan Ayres, I'm shocked to find you out on the streets with such a . . . careless driver." Her look implied she could have added worse descriptions than that.

"Yee . . . *ninny!*" Jonno had a feeling Rob, too, had stronger words in mind. "Ye're a menace, madam, on the road or off it! Ye drive a steady twenty miles per hour! Ye don't signal! And on and off the road, ye sit in judgment on everybody else!"

Mrs. Goodspeed's knuckles whitened as she clutched her purse tighter. She sniffed. She opened her mouth to speak, but then looking as much astonished as furious, she backed away. And seeming to remember that she was Grace Goodspeed, she turned, braced herself indignantly, and marched into the general store.

Jonno stared at Rob with both dismay and admiration. He shuddered to think what his grandmother would hear, but it had been awfully satisfying to see Mrs. Goodspeed silenced.

Rob, for his part, threw Jonno a keen glance without moving his head. "I take it," he said, "ye're already acquainted with the infamous Mrs. Goodspeed."

Jonno swallowed, and nodded. "She's a friend of my grandmother's."

"There's a woman," said Rob, "who's in danger of wearing out the English language single-handed. Looks like," he added, "most people are too afraid of 'er tongue to talk back." And without waiting for a reply, he snatched the battered case that held his bagpipes from the back of the jeep. "I don't suppose they're what the average thief is after, but with these I take no chances." With a last exasperated glance at Mrs. Goodspeed's tan car, Rob turned on his heel and stalked away across the parking lot.

Jonno was mystified. "Rob, what about your tobacco?"

"C'mon lad," Rob called with an eloquent toss of his head. "It's a drink I need now, not tobacco."

He was bound for Rafferty's, Jonno realized, a comfortably grungy little tavern that faced the general store. Unlike the touristy spots draped with antiseptic fishnets and cute names like The Captain's Galley, Rafferty's was a genuine, no-nonsense hangout for fishermen in search of beer, sandwiches, and the latest local wisdom. Jonno had heard his father say that "things sometimes get a little rough there toward evening." He was quite sure his parents would not want him in Rafferty's "toward evening." And meanwhile it was getting closer and closer to dinnertime.

In the middle of the parking lot, Jonno stood his ground. "Rob, I'm not sure I should go. What time do you think it is?"

"We'll check inside," said Rob firmly. "Come on, then!"

"It's not Sodom and Gomorrah, Jonno," he went on at Rafferty's door, "just a wee fisherman's pub. In Scotland, the whole neighborhood would be here at sundown, just for the company of it, bairns and all. Just one quick glass we'll have, before I run y' home."

Well, he didn't want Rob to think he was a killjoy. Or a baby. It wouldn't take that long to drink one ginger ale. And after all that marching on the beach and all that clinging to the jeep's door, he was plenty thirsty.

But as Rob shepherded him through the door of Rafferty's Jonno looked back and saw Mrs. Goodspeed marching purposefully out of the general store. She still looked furious, and she seemed to be glaring right at the door of Rafferty's Tavern.

They stepped through slanting rays of late sunshine into dimness. Rafferty's smelled of smoke and stale air, despite two ceiling fans that lazily circulated a beery breeze. Quickly Jonno was enveloped by warmth and bursts of laughter.

He blinked and began to pick out details in the gloom— a tide chart, a haggard-looking man who waved to Rob from a far barstool, a blackboard advertising special suppers in a scrawl that made his own penmanship look like an *A*-plus. From a dingy phone booth protruded the legs of a young man with a pile of coins who looked as if he had settled in for the evening. And from behind the dark, old-fashioned bar, a burly fellow with a tattoo gave Jonno a wink and Rob a grin.

"The top of the evenin' to you, Rob Loud," he called cheerfully. "What've I here that'll chase that frown?"

Rob snorted good-naturedly and walked up to the bar. "It's a Scot I am, Joe Rafferty—so none of yer Irish 'top of the evenin'.' I'll have a pint of yer infernal cold ale, and my friend here will have—what would ye like then, Jonno?"

"How about a draft root beer?" said Joe.

"Oh, that'd be great, thanks," said Jonno, who had really meant to ask for ginger ale.

"Right," said Rob. "One root beer, then, and one infernal cold ale."

"No way!" Joe's chin came up jauntily and his grin spread even wider. "No more of our bad cold brew for you! Just to demonstrate our Yankee hospitality, I got some nice warm McEwan's for you, special. Your own private stock, right under the bar here."

All the angry lines in Rob's face dissolved into a delighted grin as Joe deftly filled a mug with golden beer, drew a mug of root beer from a huge keg with a spigot, and scooped pretzels into a bowl. Jonno had never seen hands move faster, excepting maybe Rob's on the finger pipe.

"Y're a good lad, Joe," said Rob. "That was really thoughtful and I do appreciate it."

Joe looked pleased and nodded briskly. "My pleasure. Just watch out, 'cause what I'm really after is a Rafferty's pipe concert, in honor of our common Celtic ancestors."

"Aye. We'll do that one day." Rob raised his mug toward Joe. "Lang may yer lum reek, Joe Rafferty—there's a good Scots' toast for ye. . . .

"That means 'long may yer chimney smoke'—long life—but we'll let Joe wonder," he said to Jonno with a sideways wink as he handed him the basket of pretzels. "C'mon." And off he ambled to a table, in a corner where a ship's figurehead leaned out protectively like an angel in a church. "Unaccustomed as you are to pubs, ye'll be happier in a corner, which is, in any case, a great spot for sight-seein'." He touched his mug to Jonno's, as Dad often did with friends. "Here's to us, Jonno, and pity on poor twits like Grace Goodspeed who only see what's wrong with the world!"

Rob took a long swallow of warm ale and sighed with satisfaction. Jonno drank deeply through the foam of his very cold root beer. It was the best root beer he had ever had. He bit into a pretzel. Maybe what he'd taken for but-terflies in his stomach had really been hunger all along. What time could it be? It must be all right to munch a few pretzels and finish his root beer, but he wished he could be sure. If Mrs. Goodspeed had gone right home, she might have called Gram already.

As furtively as possible, Jonno dug in his pocket and sighed with relief when his fingers found three coins that might be dimes. "I think I'll just try calling home to tell them where I am," he told Rob. But now, he found, the same lanky fellow had folded his long legs into the phone booth and even shut the door.

Returning to their corner, vainly seeking a clock, Jonno discovered that one of the young men in the laughing cir-cle across the room was the lifeguard who had handed him Rob's tobacco pouch in the parking lot. What the guard and his friends were doing, though, was baffling. "Zoom! Schwartz! Boint!" It sounded like a foreign language, and abrupt enough to be an argument. But every now and then, after someone barked out something with great intensity, another would toast the group amid gales of laughter.

Rob, Jonno found, was staring at the young men, too, and his eyes looked as if someone had struck a match behind them. Catching Jonno's gaze, he smiled gently.

"It's a drinkin' game of some sort, lad. They call out quick signals, y'see, and the chap who misses his must drink up."

"Do you know the game, Rob?"

"Not this very one, but others like it. We played 'em in the pub at home, when I was those lads' age—and in England on leave before we sailed for France."

"Is it fun? It sounds crazy."

"Ah, well—crazy, aye. But a game like that tests more than how you hold your liquor. It's speed and cleverness, memory—and most of all, camaraderie."

Rob looked a little sad.

"Who did you play with?" asked Jonno.

"A bunch of lads I knew from home and then a bunch from the regiment. One lad in particular I grew up with and went off soldierin' with—he was a master . . . well, a master of everything."

"Who was he?"

"His name was Bill Ferguson. My best friend when we were growin' up."

"Where is he now?"

Rob sighed. "He's dead." After another long draft of beer, Rob touched Jonno's arm. "He's dead a long while, Jonno. He was killed on D-Day. He got his mates off the beach and then caught a stray bullet. One minute he was standin' on a rise wavin' them on, and the next he was gone. Like a light goin' out.

"But while he lived, everything he touched was golden. He not only outgrew us all, he could outswim us, outkick us in football, and outlast any man in the village at dancin'. All the lasses loved him, and the wonder of it was, the lads did, too. Incidentally, he could also drink us all under the table."

There was another roar of laughter from the young men's circle, and silence in the corner under the sheltering figurehead.

"Have I made ye sad, Jonno?"

Yes and no. It took a long time to answer. In some indefinable way, Rob's story reminded Jonno of his own father.

"I was just thinking," said Jonno at last, "that my father would have liked Bill Ferguson."

"No doubt," said Rob. "There was no one could resist him. Is he another one like that, yer father? Makes everything he touches golden?"

Jonno shrugged. "He's a Renaissance man. Someone in our newspaper said so." Finding Rob watching him intently, he began again. "That means—"

"Aye, I know. Well, that sounds a bit awesome, Jonno, but not a thing to hold against your da."

Jonno shifted in his chair and watched the foam in his root beer shrinking. "It's like I'm always trying to keep up with him, you know? At least, measure up to what he was when he was eleven."

"It could be," Rob said, "that's more in yer mind than his."

"I don't think so. He seems disappointed in me a lot."

"How 'bout yer sister?"

"I've got two, actually, and they both seem to please everybody more than I do. Well—" Jonno faltered but Rob waited patiently. "They both talk a lot more than me, and my father says I 'don't communicate.' "

Rob raised his eyebrows. "You're communin' with me pretty well."

"I know." He was surprising himself, with complaints he'd never shared. It felt good, and it felt disloyal. He wouldn't say any more.

Disconcertingly, Rob went on looking at him, and he at the table, so that neither of them noticed the bustling round lady in the checked apron until she was almost on top of them.

"Well, if it isn't himself!" she cried, bounding into their corner like a very substantial rubber ball. With surprising grace, she came to a halt beside their table, folded her ample arms, and fixed Rob with an accusing look as direct as his own. "Good evening, Rob Loud, and would you tell me please why you are filling this young person with junk that will spoil his supper?"

Rob beamed at his accuser and patted Jonno on the back. "Mary Rafferty, this is Jonathan Ayres, Jonno for short. Jonno, this lady is Joe's mother, and the chief cook and bottle-washer of this fine establishment."

"Hello, Mrs. Rafferty," said Jonno.

"I'm glad to know you, Jonno Ayres. Wouldn't you like a bowl of chowder?" She sniffed at the pretzels. "A little real nourishment?"

"What about it, Jonno?" Rob added readily. "Don't let anybody tell you people come here just to drink. Mary's chowder is the best around."

82

It sounded wonderful. Even with the pretzels, Jonno's stomach was beginning to assure him it was time for dinner. But that was all the more reason to make excuses that would remind Rob he had to leave.

"It sounds great, Mrs. Rafferty, but I'll be having dinner as soon as I get home. Thank you anyway."

Mrs. Rafferty looked not annoyed, but truly disappointed. She was clearly a nice person whose mission in life was feeding the hungry, so Jonno added, "But I hope I can come back sometime and try it."

Mary Rafferty's eyes crinkled at that and at a fresh shout from the game players. She looked fondly across the room. "If my Michael were here, God rest him, he'd be over there telling them tall stories," she said, "and if they listened to those he'd have his harmonica out next." Her glance fell on Rob's case. "If you've got your pipes, Rob, you ought to break them out for Jerry there. He's likely to miss your concert, if you ever get around to it—he's off south tomorrow to pick up his new boat, and he'll be a while bringing it back. After all these summers on our beach, a real independent lobsterman. How they do grow up!"

And off she bounded to the elbow of Jonno's lifeguard, without a shred of shyness about interrupting the organized uproar. "Here now, isn't it about time you boys thought about a little supper?"

"Rob," said Jonno, "I'm going to try calling home again."

"You can even order up a little dinner music," Mrs. Rafferty bubbled on behind him, as he threaded his way between the tables, "if you can just persuade Mr. Loud to play you a tune on his pipes. Now, what'll it be?"

The lanky caller was gone at last. In the musty phone booth, Jonno dug for his dimes and dialed Gram's number. Mounting worries about how to explain were interrupted by the maddening beep of a busy signal. It could be Peter, telling Kate that Jonno had gone off with the "freaky" piper. But perhaps Mrs. Goodspeed was already sounding her alert.

"Hey, Mr. Loud!" Across the room, Jonno's lifeguard stood up and waved enthusiastically. "We'd love to have you join us, and a little music would be a great send-off. Tom here can sing along; he's a genuine glee club tenor."

To Jonno's dismay, Rob was already drawing the pipes from the case. "Ten minutes, Jonno, and we'll be off. That's a good lad, Jerry; he deserves a tune or two for luck."

Rob began to blow through the mouthpiece, filling the bag under his arm, and a slight young man with tousled black hair rose from his seat beside Jerry and began to sing. "'Oh, ye'll take the high road, and I'll take the low road.'" His voice was light and sweet. To Jonno's surprise, Mrs. Rafferty came to attention with her hands on her hips and added a strong, clear soprano. "'And I'll be in Scotland afore ye.'" Uncertainly at first but with increasing gusto, the others joined in, with a jumble of words that became as noisy as "Zoom, Schwartz" had been before. By the time they finished, Rob stood ready to strike the pipes, and Mrs. Rafferty sashayed over to grab Jonno's hand. As she fairly danced him over to the singers, all he could think of was that he ought to be moving in the opposite direction.

"Here's one y'll all know," Rob said.

The music was penetrating in the low-ceilinged room. First to pick up the tune was Mrs. Rafferty. "'If a body meet a body, comin' through the rye . . .'" Her strong hand beat a friendly rhythm on Jonno's shoulder. "'If a body kiss a body, need a body cry?'" the dark young man sang back.

There was no deterring Mrs. Rafferty from drawing him into this fellowship of flushed and rugged faces, all turned toward Rob with pleasure. Jonno was torn, trying to remember the clock he couldn't find and forget what a good time he was having. He wouldn't have thought it possible to feel so contented and so worried, all at the same time. His senses swam. His mind was filled with music.

The song ended with another raucous crescendo, and Rob grinned at the circle around him. "Yer English words are a bit more presentable than Robbie Burns's original, but never mind." And with that, to Jonno's dismay, Joe Rafferty was at Rob's side with another mug of beer. "It's only fair," Joe said, "to pay the piper!"

"I thank you, Joe. Safe voyage, Jerry." Rob raised his mug to Jerry, but his glance took in the whole admiring circle and lastly touched on Jonno, who realized he was staring at Rob's full mug with disapproval. "Dinna worry, laddie," Rob whispered, "I've not forgotten ye." Astonishingly fast, he drank off half of his fresh beer and took the blowpipe in his mouth again. "This one's for you, Jerry," he said from the corner of his mouth.

Now this melody was familiar, and whatever it was, it brought a tear to Mrs. Rafferty's eye. By the second phrase, they were all singing again. "'Should auld acquaintance be forgot, and auld lang syne?'" It seemed to be a song about good-byes. Rob could surely choose his music.

> "And there's a hand, my trusty friend,
> And gie's a hand of thine,
> We'll take a cup o' kindness yet
> For the sake of auld lang syne."

By the time two or three verses and choruses of that were done, even Jerry and his friends were blinking suspiciously. As Rob finished, Joe clapped him on the back and everyone cheered, as if to turn the bittersweetness back to celebration.

"I'd love to go on," said Rob, "but I'm about played out for today and my friend here needs to get home for supper."

"You come back, Jonno." Mrs. Rafferty put a hand on Jonno's head. "Don't forget I owe you some chowder."

"Thanks, Mrs. Rafferty. I wonder," said Jonno, unsure he really wanted to hear, "if anybody knows what time it is?"

Joe Rafferty shrugged and wagged his thumb at an unusually clean spot on the wall behind him. "We sent Dad's old chiming clock out for repair when it got to running more than an hour off true time. If it comes back really accurate," he chuckled, "we won't know what to do with ourselves!"

But one of Jerry's friends tugged at the wrist of his gray sweatshirt. "Ahh—it's nearly seven-thirty."

Jonno's spirits fell to the soles of his sneakers. This was what came of wild surmise. Mrs. Goodspeed must have reported long ago, and if that were not enough, he was almost surely late for dinner. Even if his whereabouts were known, that would be an offense against his grandmother's efficient scheduling. It would be nice, he thought wistfully, to live like the Raffertys, who could tolerate an eccentric clock.

One look at Jonno's distress, and Rob drained his mug. He scooped up his case and they hustled again through the stained-glass doors to the parking lot. This time, old Maudie leaped alive. "Aha!" said Rob. "I'll have you home in two shakes of a lamb's tail!"

Jonno couldn't help smiling as they managed to leave the parking lot by the exit.

Rob shot him a sidelong glance. "They're sticklers about schedules, are they? Yer folks?"

"Well, my father hates being late—himself, or anyone else. But when we're staying with Gram, it's extra sticky."

Rob chuckled and shook his head. "That's enough to give us old folks a bad name."

"What my mom says is, Gram's talented but prickly." Like her son, Jonno added to himself.

They were quiet then, like the road home, which was cool, gray, and empty. Jonno huddled on the lumpy seat, vaguely aware that the evening was getting cool and he could use a sweatshirt. Much more bothersome was his state of mind. He was frantic to get home, but dreaded it. Rafferty's had been wonderful, but disturbing—and not in any way that Gram and Mrs. Goodspeed would have expected. He turned over the thought that their good time in the pub had been oddly like one of his father's stories.

As they reached the rise before the ocean, Rob looked at him again. "Ye're quiet, Jonno. Are y' frettin', or was it too much for you, all that talk of auld lang syne?"

Jonno thought of Mrs. Rafferty's bounce and the young men's cheers. He smiled and shook his head. "I've got a question though. What exactly is 'auld lang syne'?"

"It means 'old long ago.' The words're from an ancient song that Burns wrote down 'n' then the thing was set to other music."

The jeep turned onto the road along the bluff, and Jonno said, "You talk about Robert Burns . . . and your friend Bill . . . as if they were alive for you now, no matter when they lived or died."

Rob cocked his head thoughtfully. "Well, when you get to my age, the past's right with you. It's not sad to me now, y'see, Bill and all that. The storyin', the rememberin'—it's how you keep 'em with you."

"Who?"

"Why—the people you've loved. And even," Rob added with a chuckle, "the people who were truly terrible."

The jeep braked suddenly as they reached the entrance to Gram's lane. The road to the Farnums' stretched in the opposite direction.

"Don't turn, Rob." If there was going to be a scene, he'd like to keep Rob out of it. "I can run about as fast as the jeep can take these ruts."

"But I could come down and tell your da it's my fault, yer bein' late."

"That's okay." To settle the question, Jonno opened the

jeep door and scrambled out his side. Rob leaned across the front seat and held out his right hand.

"Well, there's a hand, my trusty friend," he rumbled.

Jonno took Rob's hand and nodded. "Thanks. For the root beer, Rob, and all the music. And the stories."

Rob's gray eyes shone in the dusk. "Good luck with the dragons."

The light shining from Gram's windows onto her tubs of geraniums should have been welcoming, but Jonno skirted the bright pools like a burglar looking for the safest point of entry. He hoped to judge the temper of the household by gliding past open windows, but he was frustrated. There were only kitchen sounds, unthreatening, and Gram's voice, ominous, announcing her intention to put something back in the oven. Well, what sort of barrage could there be, when the target wasn't yet in sight?

By the breezeway that led into the kitchen, Pippin startled up from a snooze with a few tentative, flustered woofs. "Shh, Pip!" Jonno dropped to one knee in the dry grass and gave the dog a hug that muffled apologetic whines and whimpers. "You don't hafta worry; I won't tell anyone I caught you napping." Pip licked his ear and Jonno hugged him tighter. "You're the one I needed to talk to. It's too bad dogs can't answer phones."

"Jonathan! Do you know what time it is?"

With a rough, warm tongue massaging one ear, he hadn't heard his father's step. Phil Ayres's eyes were steely, his voice tight and level, devoid of its normal exuberance. Most disquieting of all was his deliberate coolness, scarier than other people's explosions.

"You come home this late and hang around out here

playing with the dog?" The voice was mild, cold, sarcastic. His father seemed as angry as Jonno had ever seen him.

"Dad, I just got here. I'm sorry I'm late."

"I presume you did notice that the sun was going down."

This sparring with words was confusing, especially because nothing was being said about Rafferty's or Grace Goodspeed. Was it possible she hadn't called? Jonno had a moment of optimism. Maybe Gram's phone was out of order. Or Mrs. Goodspeed's. Maybe by tomorrow Mrs. Goodspeed would forget the whole thing. Sure, said a more reasonable part of Jonno's brain. Or maybe we'll have a blizzard.

"I said," his father repeated, "I presume you did notice the sun was going down."

Jonno despaired of dealing with his father's sarcasm. A clever reply would sound rude, even if he had one, so he looked at his sneakers and said nothing.

"Well!" said his father brusquely. "Dinner has already been delayed long enough. Kate found out from Peter that you'd gone up the beach with the piper. But I hope you have something reasonable to say about where you've been so long."

So at Gram's trestle table Jonno faced a platter of tired-looking corn, a slab of cooling bluefish, and a circle of frowns. Pip, whose usual mealtime strategy was to lie on Jonno's feet and hope for downward-drifting morsels, ambled off to sleep in front of the stone fireplace. Deserting the scene of battle, Jonno thought gloomily. Only Alison, round-eyed and curious, looked almost sympathetic.

Kate was fairly bouncing with impatience. "I don't care

91

where you were!" she stormed. "My stomach feels like the Grand Canyon, and I just want some supper!"

"I don't know what you were thinking of, Jonno," said his mother. His father's calling him "Jonathan" had signaled disaster, and his mother's "Jonno" spelled trouble with her, too. "Here's the freshest bluefish we've had in a year; I waited till the last minute to put it in the oven, and we're eating it lukewarm anyway!"

What was so important, anyway, about a piece of bluefish, compared with having an adventure or making a friend? As if she'd monitored his thoughts, his mother went on, "It's not the bluefish; it's the principle—of being together to eat it, of your having the consideration to let us know if something gets in the way."

She'd have said more, Jonno thought, but she didn't want to make a debate of dinner. More odd and ominous was his grandmother's stony silence. Like Grace Goodspeed, Gram normally seemed to view a gap in a conversation as a breach of etiquette. Usually her chatter fluttered like a moth around the edges of any awkward silence. But now she sat as quiet as the fierce-looking ancestors whose portraits hung in her Boston dining room, as quiet and as disapproving.

Jonno glanced sideways at his father, who seemed absorbed in stowing away his bluefish as efficiently as possible. Now he wished he had braved the sarcasm, back in the driveway, and just tried to explain straight out that, after his walk with Colonel Farnum's piper, things had gotten unexpectedly complicated. Jonno clenched his fists in his lap and could feel himself drawing inward. He hated arguments, and even more he hated the prospect of arguing about an experience he hadn't yet sorted out for himself.

Once when he was small he had gone to the inlet with his father on a gray day at low tide. They hadn't meant to walk so far, just rambled along watching the terns dive and Pip scuttle ahead and back, a lanky puppy getting his first savor of the sea. Just when Jonno was realizing that his legs were very tired indeed, they had come on the farthest shelf of beach with the outward rush of the tide before them, and his father had hoisted him onto his shoulders and waded out to a sandbar. Serendipity, Phil Ayres declared it, for the bar was covered with more whole shells than were ever likely on the ocean beach.

His father had scooped up a whole rainbow of scallop shells, but one special moon shell Jonno had found himself and carried back in the kangaroo pocket of his sweatshirt, chortling on his father's shoulders and peeking every little while to be sure his treasure was still safe. He felt the same way now about Rob Loud, though he wasn't sure yet why the man seemed so special. It was more than the bagpipe. Jonno wanted to tuck their hours in some private corner of his mind until he could turn them over and over and understand what they meant to him.

His father had finished his bluefish and seemed to be busy attacking an ear of corn, but he laid it down abruptly and looked directly into Jonno's eyes. "Look, Jonno," he said, "anybody can lose track of time. But you know you're expected to tell us when you're going to take off somewhere. And what makes me really angry—as usual—is your lack of communication."

Jonno felt held, hypnotized by his father's accusing

look. As so often happened with his father, it seemed safer to say nothing. There had been a moment to speak, back in the driveway, so maybe, as Rob said, the problem was in his own mind, in his conviction that he wasn't clever enough to make his father understand.

Still, he knew what was going to happen. Quite aside from Mrs. Goodspeed, whose silence couldn't last forever, he was trapped by his own honesty, his father's anger, and the reproach in his mother's eyes. He had tried a few fibs in his day, but he was really terrible at lying. Even other kids could look at him hard and tell he was a fraud.

Still wishing this conversation wouldn't happen, he began, "We walked up to the inlet, Mr. Loud and I . . ."

"Loud!" Kate hooted with laughter. "I can't believe that's really his name!"

Jonno glared at her across the table. Her green eyes danced. Unfortunately, a little food had quickly revived her interest in his business. "You think that's funny?" he asked, trying to keep his tone as cool as his father's.

"Of course I think it's funny! It's so appropriate! And Peter said . . ." A fit of giggles erupted, and Kate pounded the table gently as if to squelch them.

"What did Peter say?" He was having a lot of trouble sounding cool.

Kate giggled again. "Oh, he called the bagpipe 'a wheezin' sheepskin.' " She managed to turn another giggle into more of a hiccup. "And he said the piper went up the beach 'squeezin' and wheezin'.' I thought," she said, looking faintly apologetic but still chuckling, "that was pretty creative."

94

"That's enough, Kate," their father said, turning to Jonno.

"Then, Mr. Loud said he'd drive me home after he got tobacco at the general store."

Gram was on him in an instant.

"I don't know why your parents are being so subtle, Jonno; it's not as if we don't know where you were! It's just unfortunate Grace Goodspeed was delayed on her way home and left your poor mother worrying. Till twenty minutes ago, we all thought you might have drowned!

"Now, of course," she went on with increasing vehemence, "I'm merely mortified! You can be sure that what delayed Grace Goodspeed was stopping to let Sarah Hopkins know what my grandson's been up to. How you could—"

"Please, Mother," said Phil Ayres firmly, "I want to hear what Jonno has to say for himself."

Gram still peppered. "How you could go traipsing off with a ruffian who drives like a maniac!"

"He doesn't drive like a maniac," Jonno shot back without thinking. "Mrs. Goodspeed does, though."

"Jonno!" As Gram looked outraged, his father's voice grew tighter than ever. "I want to know why you never told us you were going off to the store, and I want to know how you ended up at Rafferty's."

Jonno gave up all hope of wanting to finish dinner and set down his fork, taking care not to let it clatter. "I didn't ask about going to the store because I thought we'd be back in the time it would take to get permission. Then

Rob—Mr. Loud—kind of marched me over to Rafferty's after he got mad at Mrs. Goodspeed. And I tried to call from there, a couple of times, but first Rafferty's phone wasn't free, and then Gram's line was busy."

His parents exchanged one of their looks, and his mother spoke as if she were sorting the words to discard the ones with rough edges. "I do think, Jonathan, that a man of his age and . . . um . . . sophistication . . . might be on the beach because he wants to be alone. And if Rafferty's is his idea of an outing, he's probably not the ideal companion for an eleven-year-old boy."

Jonno was beginning to feel less fearful than angry in his own right. "But, Mom, all I did there was drink root beer and listen to 'Auld Lang Syne'!"

His father gave him a quizzical look. "So, Jonno, what is this piper like?"

"Well, he's great," said Jonno slowly. "Mostly he told me stories and I listened while he played the pipes."

"Squeezin' and wheezin'!" Kate's shoulders shook silently despite a withering look from her father.

Gram cocked her head to one side and looked at Jonno like an irate sparrow. "I can't imagine spending all those hours with a man who can't even be civil to Grace Goodspeed!"

"He was civil to me," Jonno said quietly. "He knows a lot about poetry, Dad." Jonno hoped that would make it clear that Mr. Loud was more presentable than Gram's spies implied. Instead, his father's face darkened.

"That's hardly an explanation." The threatening sort of quiet was back in his voice. "I know a lot about poetry,

Jonno. But I don't recall your talking to me for three hours lately."

His mother reached out and touched his father's hand.

His father glanced at her, then back at Jonno, and shook his head. "I'm concerned, Jonno. First because of what Mom said—you might be a nuisance to this man, without meaning to, and he'd be too tactful to say so—though from his reputation, a surplus of tact doesn't seem to be a problem. More importantly, we really know almost nothing about him. Until I know more, I'm not sure he's the best person for you to be wandering a lonely beach with. Let alone hanging out in Rafferty's."

"I thought he was a nice man," said Alison in an unusually small voice.

Her brave bit of moral support and the injustice of what his father had said made Jonno bolder than usual. "Dad, you always say not to prejudge people," he cried. "What about Snively and Snitko, all your great characters from the navy? Isn't spending time with someone the best way to learn more about him?" He could feel the flush rising in his cheeks as he talked.

His father's voice hardened in response to Jonno's challenge. "I was twenty-three when I knew those men, Jonno; you're eleven! What I'm saying is that you're not ever to wander off with him again for indeterminate lengths of time or without our having any idea where you are! If Mr. Loud wants your company, you can arrange to get together ahead of time so your mother and I know what is going on."

Jonno thought of the methodical Weekly Planner on his

father's study desk at home, and his heart sank. "But, Dad, he doesn't seem to have a nice, neat life like ours. I just don't think he's an appointment sort of person!"

"I don't want to argue about this, Jonno," said his father sharply. "I'm not sure I want you with him at all. I have to think about it. You think he's pretty unpredictable, do you?"

"Unpredictable or unreliable, it's all the same!" Gram declared piously.

For the first time in his life, Jonno resented his grandmother. Unpredictable was not the same as unreliable, he was certain, and he was sure his father knew that, too. For the first time his family seemed not only unexplainable but unbearable. He could feel tears of frustration starting behind his eyes, and he wasn't going to cry in front of Kate. His chair hit the floor with a bang as he leaped up and headed for his room in the loft.

He paused at the door just long enough to absorb his father's last words. "You're not to see him again, Jonathan, without my permission!"

From his bunk in the loft, Jonno stared out at the Big Dipper. He felt as if they had dumped his moon shell on Gram's table underneath a glaring light and gloated over flaws he hadn't seen in the world of seagrass, sand, and water.

Didn't they know he was old enough to make some judgments about people? Well, he'd have to avoid needing to lie outright because he was so bad at it, but he was also old enough to have some secrets.

He might not be able to see Rob again on his father's terms. But he was going to see him anyway.

A gull's scream woke him.

The alarm clock on the sea chest said 5:55, so it was morning, even though Jonno felt as if he had never really slept at all. His eyes, his mouth, his brain felt fuzzy. The night had been a crazy quilt of dreams: a piper in blue jeans leading some soldiers over a sand dune; Gram and Grace Goodspeed bent over lobster pots on a bobbing boat, with Dad repeating, "Not without my permission."

No gull sailed in the square of sky he could see from his window. Maybe that too had been part of a dream. But from the yard Pip gave a few grumbly barks that convinced Jonno there was no further point in trying to sleep. He had thinking to do before he faced anyone, even Rob, and fresh air might help. Last night, on the verge of sleep, he had begun a mental list of his assorted worries in order of importance, and even that had been a muddle. So right now, in the clothes he'd lain down in last night, he'd take Pip for a run on the beach, before anyone could tell him he had to have permission for that, too.

Jonno closed the loft door gently, called Pip quietly as he pulled on his sweatshirt, and padded up the lane munching on a chocolate bar from his emergency rations. It was satisfying, this morning, to think that he was not having what Gram would call "a perfectly balanced breakfast."

There'd been talk at Rafferty's of storms later in the week, but as they pounded down the wooden steps the sun hung just above the horizon like a golden ball and flooded sea and inlet with light. Rounding the cove, Jonno reflected that he ought to get up early more often. He felt blessedly, peacefully alone. And then he realized that in the very hollow at the dunes' crest where he and Pip had crouched in the fog listening, Rob Loud was standing, tuning up his pipes.

Jonno couldn't imagine not being glad to see Rob, but he was not ready to talk about his father's ultimatum. So he would have to find what his history teacher, describing some battle, had called "a diversionary tactic." He would talk about anything except last night.

By the time Pip and Jonno were halfway up the path through the beach grass, Rob was sitting on a sand rise fiddling mysteriously with the longest pipe. As Pip raced for him, Jonno watched the man's head come up, his wary air become delight. The look of him reminded Jonno of a seascape lit with scudding patterns of sun and shadow.

No hint of bleakness, though, was in the voice that rumbled, "It's Jonathan Ayres, is it, and furry friend as well!

"Y're an early bird, this mornin'," Rob went on. "Or have ye just been banished due to last night's escapade?"

Diversionary tactic. Jonno shrugged. "You're early, too. I didn't expect to see anyone now but fishermen."

"Aye. I didn't sleep well myself; my leg's been twingin'," Rob said lightly. "But tell me, did y' make yer peace at home, then?"

Diversionary tactic. Jonno stared down at the pipes that sprawled over Rob's knees like a tired octopus. Yesterday he'd been too deep in Rob's words and music to look closely at the pipes themselves. Now, spread out in the high, clear light of morning, they shone like some exotic creation from a pirate's chest—gleaming dark, glowing white, glistening silver.

"Cat got yer tongue?" Rob's voice was gentle, but the glance he gave Jonno's rumpled, day-old clothes was sharp and curious. Then he followed Jonno's gaze and pointed with a sinewy forefinger. "That's blackwood from Africa, the best for piping—aged for years before the instrument was put together. Ivory from Africa, too, and silver from who knows where. The bag's good Scottish sheepskin. A patchwork of the best there is—the piper's version of a fiddler's Stradivarius!"

Jonno laid a finger on a satiny length of wood. "Has this a name?"

"Drones, Jonno, these pipes that ride the shoulder. Each sounds one steady note below the tune that's played on the finger pipe, the chanter. The shorter drones," Rob pointed, "are tenors, pitched an octave lower than the chanter's low A. The longest drone," Rob lowered his voice comically, "is a bass like me, and plays an A still lower."

Intrigued in spite of himself, Jonno wished he had listened better in music class, and Rob grinned at him as if he read his mind.

"Is this more than you really wanted to know?" Rob asked.

Jonno shook his head. What it was, was an unexpectedly interesting diversionary tactic. "So I hear two other notes, like other voices when you play a tune, and that's why it sounds like a chorus?"

Rob reached out with his free hand and tousled Jonno's already tumbled hair. "Y've a good ear, Jonno," he said. " 'Chorus' is an apt word. If you hear that, ye'll like an odd thing about the pipes: The best way to teach them's with the voice. A master piper chantin' sounds eerily like the pipes themselves."

That sounded suspiciously easy, Jonno thought. Maybe there was hope even for a certified musical klutz like Jonathan Ayres. "You mean," he asked, "you can just hum a tune at a person and he'll know how to play it?"

But Rob gave him a mischievous grin. "It's less of a hum than a chant, called *canterach*. And what it'll tell is how the thing *should* sound. Learning to play it that way might take a few years," he chuckled.

"That sounds depressing," said Jonno with conviction. "That's a lot longer than it took me to learn to play baseball!"

A silver-frosted eyebrow shot up to meet Rob's stubborn thatch of hair, and the look he gave Jonno was appraising. "But surely ye've a few things left to learn about baseball? A few years yet before ye're ready for the Yanks or the Red Stockings?

"Most worthwhile things take time, y'know, Jonno. The great thing about bein'—eleven is it, or twelve—is ye've years and years for doin' things ye've not even begun to think of!"

And the rotten thing, thought Jonno silently, is that you're expected to think like a grown-up while still being treated like a little kid. "Being eleven isn't all that great, Rob," he said.

"Aye, well, my advice is to enjoy it. 'Nae man can tether time nor tide,' said my old chum Robert Burns. You can be sure of gettin' older soon enough!"

As if Rob had heard the bitter ring in his own voice, he brushed his gray hair back from his forehead with an impatient thrust of his right hand and settled himself into a more comfortable slouch against the dune. "So tell me what it is you like about baseball, Jonno."

Jonno shrugged wordlessly. The guys he played ball with didn't worry about why they played the game. Doug and Mickey just took it for granted that liking it was the normal thing to do. They'd probably think Jonno was weird if they knew he had a sort of philosophy about it, so he had never discussed it with anyone before. But Rob was giving him an amused, relentless stare.

"Well." Jonno wrapped his arms around his knees. "It's not that I never make mistakes. But it's not a jumble like some other games. When the ball comes to you, it's like being in the zoom lens of a camera. You're there, and the ball's there, and you've just that instant to get it all together."

The corners of Rob's mouth twitched. "Ah. It's rhythmic then. Precise." His eyes glinted. "A lot like piping."

Jonno ducked his head and smiled at himself, on the spot again. "But baseball comes naturally to me. At least, it did till lately."

"Aye." Rob sounded serious suddenly. "About last night, lad . . ."

Time for another diversion. Sunshine fell like a spot-

103

light on the bagpipe's silver fittings, and Jonno spoke as if his last thought had been left unfinished. "But even if a bat is more my thing," he said, "that's sure some instrument."

Rob's eyes were keener suddenly. "I still want to know about last night, Jonno, but I first must tell you this is some instrument and more." His voice rang in the soft air. "It's a regular historical personage, the bagpipe, and a storyteller without equal! Why, these pipes are woven into history as tightly as the squares and stripes that make a tartan."

Rob pushed himself to his feet and clambered stiffly to the top of the nearest dune. He turned in a circle to survey the beach and inlet. His voice was still rising.

"Suppose," he called, "I'm a piper captured in battle, held in the clammy keep of a castle by the sea." Eyes kindling, he swept his right arm across the line of the horizon and swung it back to point at Jonno. "Ye're scout for a boatload of my clansmen, come to free me from durance vile, and maybe capture the enemy chieftain, too."

Jonno unwound his legs and knelt in the hollow, letting Rob's imagination wash over him. He felt less like a clansman than like one of Cooper's Indians in the prow of a canoe. But just as it had yesterday, his heart told him it was the mood that mattered.

"What you don't know," Rob called again, "is that this sly fox of a chieftain has called down a raft of cousins from the hills, to reinforce the castle guard."

"What can we do?" Jonno called back. He was surprised by the urgency of his own imagining.

"I've got to warn ye off," Rob cried. "Ye're far outnumbered and the tide's about to turn against ye! So"—he reeled a bit atop the dune, swatting at a dragonfly that hovered—"I first convince the laird that I'll go mad if I can't parade the pipes along his parapets."

In the hollow, Jonno planted one foot before him as if he were steadying himself in a rocking boat, and stroked with an oar that existed only in their minds. "We're comin', Rob, we're comin' on the tide!" His voice was rising, too. "How can you stop us? There'll be a brave but bloody battle. We're full of . . . wild surmise!" he yelled against the breeze.

Rob nodded with satisfaction and hurtled on with the story. "Thank heaven for *canterach*, then, for it's about to save yer hide! My only weapon's pipin' you a warnin', with piper's chantin' turned inside out. Your mission now's to speed away with silent oars, and live to fight another day." Rob gestured grandly toward the bay behind Jonno's back. "Now! Row! Fly!"

Rob struck the pipes and eerie, agitated voices rang across the hollow. Pippin flattened himself in the sand with worried eyes, but Jonno barely noticed. He could almost feel the present fall away. The year and century as well. He flung himself back in the sand, dug in his bare heels and stroked the air as if to clear a moonlit bay, and then he sat quite still, forearms dangling across his knees, and simply watched the piper.

The tall figure on the sandhill beside him might well belong on a castle wall. With the climbing sun behind him, Rob's faded denim shirt and serviceable khakis were obscured by shadow. Silhouetted against the glare of beach and sky with wailing pipes and wind-whipped hair, he seemed a vision from another time.

He played to a shrieking finale and thrust his right fist

overhead in a cheer. "Ye did it, lad! Hurrah! Ye're free!" he hollered.

Unexplainable but unmistakable joy welled up in Jonno. With an answering whoop he threw his arms to the sky and fell back spread-eagled in the sand.

He stared into the everlasting bowl of sky with a sense of having just come back from somewhere far away. Gone were the scratchy cobwebs of the night and the frustrations of the family. Here with Rob, he could say anything, imagine anything, and be himself without apologies. Here he was free.

This was more than make-believe. More like a revelation. Yet Rob was laughing as he shambled down the dune and sat above Jonno—an earthy laugh that rolled on like surf and made Jonno laugh back.

"Most fun I've had in a decade or so," Rob declared, shaking his head.

Jonno just lay smiling, reluctant to admit the spell was broken. Then abruptly he raised his head. "But did you make that up, Rob, or did it really happen?"

Rob shrugged. "It's hard to say. The tale's been told for generations." Rob hesitated. "Another version says the enemy clan had its piper too, who also understood the message."

"So what did he do?" Jonno sat up eagerly.

"Told the laird," said Rob flatly, watching Jonno's face.

"And what did he do?"

"Had the piper's fingers cut off, so he couldn't send more messages."

Jonno gulped. Even Peter might be impressed by that one.

"It's not an occupation without hazards," Rob added drily. "The pipes have ruffled lots of feathers, one way or other. Ye begin to see why they were banned, after Culloden."

"Culloden?" Sometimes talking with Rob was a little like being lost in a library.

"Culloden was that battle Charlie lost."

Rob's eyes looked as cloudy with memories as if he had been there himself, and Jonno felt again as if time were slipping out of joint. His scalp prickled.

"Who banned the pipes?"

"The British. As an instrument of war, inciting to rebellion." Rob patted the pipes lying in his lap. "Not for nothing is this called the Great Highland Warpipe. Believe me, Jonno, music has power! It can be a gentlin' thing, or a potent weapon. All you've heard is a lone piper." His right hand swept the air. "If you heard a hundred, playin' in perfect unison with their plaids blowin' in the wind, you'd know what I mean!"

Jonno stared into Rob's gray eyes and believed him utterly. Jonno could picture him, lean as now but lithe and young, striding over a green moor in a mass of skirling pipes.

"It's a sound to curl yer hair, Jonno," Rob went on. "It's enough to make yer grandmother grab a claymore and follow the pipes to hell!"

No.

"Not *my* grandmother!" Jonno blurted, and Rob threw back his head in a peal of laughter.

But Jonno stared at the fists he'd clenched, remembering last night. Anger seeped back as he thought of his grandmother's unfairness and his father's ultimatum. He was risking another row with his father just by being here with Rob, although he hadn't planned this meeting. Was he now expected to run home and report? Worst of all, how could he tell Rob they must meet by appointment only?

Rob pushed himself off the side of the dune and settled in the sand hollow, so that they were face-to-face. "I guess I should have said 'enough to make *my* grandmother rally round the flag.' " More gently he added, as Jonno failed to meet his eyes, "There's a problem, is there, with yer gram? Maybe it's time we talked about last night."

"Mmm," said Jonno reluctantly. He had run out of diversionary tactics. He took a deep breath. "There was some trouble when I got home last night. We're staying at Gram's house, and Mrs. Goodspeed is a pretty good friend of hers."

"So the grapevine was at work before you got there?"

"Yup."

"They were really angry."

A statement rather than a question, it made Jonno look at Rob directly again. He nodded. He might as well get it all out, now that he'd begun. "My dad wants me to ask permission if I'm going to be with you."

Rob looked at him intently. "So already you may be in more trouble?" Jonno nodded, shook his head, nodded again, felt a sting behind his eyes, and regretted the lack of a loft to escape to. "But surely they know people run into one another on a beach?"

There was a sad sort of silence in the hollow. Surf murmured; gulls cried.

"Well, then," said Rob more briskly, rising, "I'll be off, and you'd best get back before ye're missed. Is yer gram's name Ayres? Is her number in the directory?"

All those wonderfully tangled *r*'s.

Jonno sighed, and nodded. He should never have told Rob. It would change everything.

"Jonathan Ayres." Rob spoke in a stern sort of voice that Jonno hadn't heard from him before. "I'll ring you up." And he turned and paced stiffly out of the hollow and off down the beach.

Jonno watched until Rob was a small figure trailing wild music against a distant ruffle of surf. In a way he does have ghosts with him, Jonno thought. Squinting Patrick. Bonnie Prince Charlie. And all those pipers who've marched over moors in his long life and lives before.

Ring me up, thought Jonno. When he's free as the wind to come and go. Will he ever ring me up? I doubt it.

"Come on, Jonno. We'll just hit some balls."

It wasn't so much an invitation as an announcement. Since his father had put on tennis whites to eat his breakfast cereal, it was clear to Jonno that he had the morning planned.

Jonno's tone was the lightest he could manage. "Dad, isn't it kind of hot?"

It would be another day like yesterday, he knew from the heat that had ambushed him and Pip on the bluff as they came up from the beach. And the tennis courts were three miles inland. But heat was not their most forbidding quality. A tennis court, to Jonno, was like a foreign country, complete with arbitrary rules and illogical language. A country ruled by his father, where he bumbled around, overstepping boundaries, frustrated by decorum.

"We'll go right now, while it's still relatively cool," said his father quietly.

"Dad, you know I can't play tennis!" Jonno knew his reasonable tone was faltering. "You'd even have more fun with Mom . . ."

"Even!" His mother's eyes were laughing, but she feigned insult as she went on scrambling eggs. "As it happens, I've had to forfeit today's match with Navratilova because my tennis elbow's acting up again!" She brandished a plate of eggs for Jonno and murmured to him as he came to fetch it, "Besides, it's been a while since you and Dad had any time alone. I think he'd like to iron out what happened last night."

That could be worse than a tennis lesson, Jonno thought, but his father sounded calm, almost soothing.

"You know, Jonno, your main trouble with tennis is that you try too hard. You can't go at it with the same slug-for-the-fence attitude that works in baseball. You need to relax, go for a little more finesse." (And we all know how loaded with relaxed finesse I am, thought Jonno.) "And that just comes with experience. You just have to keep trying."

"Most worthwhile things take time," Rob had told him only hours ago. An age ago, it seemed, before this family's rules had sent Rob up the beach alone. Coming from Rob, the admonition had sounded like wisdom with a hint of mystery. Coming from his father, the same advice seemed preachy, predictable, and aggravating. Maybe Rob's thoughts sounded better because they always seemed to seek response. His preference for Rob, rather than two hours spent with him without permission, was making Jonno feel quite guilty.

So, out of guilt, he said, "Okay—I'll try."

They were just closing the car doors when Kate hallooed her way out of the house behind them.

"Yoohoo, Daddy! Peter's on the phone—could we hitch a ride to the tennis courts with you? If we hurry?"

Phil Ayres threw up his hands and nodded, but sat back with a small sigh of exasperation as Kate ran back inside.

111

Jonno was surprised to see that his father looked truly disappointed.

"Jonno, I've got nothing against Kate and Peter, but I was really hoping we could go alone."

Jonno didn't know what to say. He certainly couldn't say that he was relieved despite Peter's probable teasing about Rob.

"I don't suppose you're too pleased about what's happening with Kate and Peter," his father went on.

Again Jonno didn't know what to say, so he shrugged. "It's okay," he said. "It really doesn't matter."

"Well, the main thing I wanted to say," said his father hastily as Peter careened his bike to a halt by the breezeway, "is that you probably felt ganged-up-on last night, and if so, I'm sorry. I didn't mean for it to happen that way."

Jonno looked into his father's eyes and felt a little warmth growing in the empty, aching place he had discovered when Rob walked out of the dunes playing the pipes.

The screen door slammed behind Kate. "Thanks for waiting, Dad."

"Hi, Mr. Ayres."

His father smiled despite his thwarted plan, perhaps because Peter was grinning foolishly at Kate as usual. "Peter, you look good with that racket. I'm glad to see you're taking up a thinking man's game!"

"Hey, Jonno, how's the piper's shadow?"

"Hi, Pete." Now it starts, thought Jonno. But he detected a warning frown from Kate that squelched Peter's teasing, or at least distracted him. For he surely was distracted. Glancing backwards throughout the drive to town, Jonno decided that, unless Peter had perfected a technique of incredible subtlety, he had even given up scoping. Well, it really was okay about him and Kate, Jonno thought, as they passed the general store and Rafferty's, shuttered in the morning sunlight. What was important to Peter really didn't matter to him anymore. What mattered was that his father seemed to be relenting this morning. That made even the prospect of a tennis lesson bearable.

To Jonno's relief, the newer courts in the park had been claimed by squadrons of earnest and already overheated players. But the lumpier trio of courts, hidden behind the school, lay quiet, baking in the sun—doubly lucky, for they could leave the center court as buffer. He and Kate played such erratic tennis that they could use as many barricades as possible.

"Have fun, kids." His father waved Kate and Peter toward the far court and began his limbering up ritual. "You might do a few stretches, too, Jonno."

Absently, Jonno swung his racket around his shoulders like a batter warming up, and watched Peter using his to mock-dribble a tennis ball across the middle court. He felt not all there, as if his mind were still on the beach with Rob. Even if he thought there was no sense to a game where "love" meant "nothing," he had to pull himself together. If his father was having second thoughts about last night's ultimatum, the best thing he could do would be to try really hard at this tennis. He'd ignore the heat already shimmering on the court's surface, and be as attentive and mature as he could be. His racket swung more purposefully.

"Now, Jonno," said his father as he bounced some used

113

balls tentatively, "try to remember what I said at breakfast. Just take it easy. You're quick to begin with, and in tennis you always have more time than you think. So concentrate on rhythm, form, meeting the ball. You don't have to kill it; just keep it in play."

His father backed away from the net and gently stroked a ball, perfectly placed for Jonno's forehand. Follow it as closely as a baseball leaving the bat, Jonno thought. Get the racket back; meet it; follow through. Miraculously, the ball returned almost to the spot from which his father had hit it.

Deftly, his father returned the ball to Jonno's backhand. Already testing, Jonno thought. He turned, shifted his grip on the racket, planted his feet but not quite in time, and the ball thunked into the net.

"You have to anticipate"—there was an embarrassed whoop from Kate and Peter's court, and his father lobbed their stray ball back without missing a syllable—"a little more."

By the end of half an hour, Jonno was hot enough to feel vaguely dizzy, and his right hand hurt from gripping the racket so intently. He had counted ten balls hit out of bounds and five into the net, but that was minor compared with the sidewinding barrage that came from Kate.

"These," Peter declared, juggling three optic yellow balls as he and Jonno retrieved strays from the middle court, "are Kate Ayres's UFOs. That's to say," he hollered as he pocketed two and made conjuring gestures at Kate with the other, "they are—for Kate Ayres—Uncontrollable Flying Objects."

Jonno grinned at Peter, and Kate cheerfully stuck out her tongue at both of them.

"Jonno." As he jogged back onto their court, his father beckoned him to the net. Phil Ayres looked relaxed and pleased, but sweat stood on his forehead and trickled down his forearms. "You were right about the heat."

The back of Jonno's neck was beginning to prickle from the sun. "Maybe," he said hopefully, "we should quit and go to the beach."

"Not yet." His father shook his head and drops of sweat flew. "You seem to be getting the hang of this for the first time, and I want you to try some serves. Use those balls you collected, and I'll hit you a few more. Oh—and Jonno," he added offhandedly, as Jonno turned away, "there was something else I meant to say about last night."

In midstride, Jonno caught himself and swung back toward his father, raspy palm and prickly neck forgotten. Maybe the sunrise time with Rob had been an omen, a hint that today would free him from his troubles. Kate and Peter were acting mellow, he hadn't done anything really bizarre on the tennis court, and maybe now his father was going to say that last night had been a misunderstanding.

"I haven't forgotten what I told you," said his father quietly, "and I don't want you to forget it either. But I'll ask around. I'll make some inquiries."

Jonno's head pounded as if the sun had been switched off briefly and then turned to double power. "Inquiries?"

"About your Mr. Loud."

About Rob, who hated gossip.

"Oh, Dad, please don't. You can't do that."

His father squinted. His partly hidden eyes were piercing green and totally assured. "I'll be tactful."

"But . . ."

His father tossed his head and turned on his heel. "Jonno," he said over his shoulder, "just serve."

Jonno turned, too, and carried his stupid clutch of stupid balls back to the baseline. Everything he wore was drenched with sweat. Inside and out, he felt as if he were drowning. He made a little show of twitching his wet shirt off his neck and shoulders, moving deliberately, trying for composure.

He looked across the net at his father. Tall, strong, nonchalant, apparently unaware of having just made his son sick to his stomach. "Just serve." He'd like to drill a ball right down his throat. Was this what hate felt like?

Jonno picked up the first ball. "Just serve." He'd show him.

His racket met the first toss too high and drove the ball completely off the court.

"Jonno! Take it easy!" called his father cheerfully.

His racket met the second toss with a satisfying snap, but the ball boomeranged back from the tape on the net, loud and ineffectual.

"Now you're overcompensating." The coach was sounding a bit impatient.

The third serve was into the net. And the next. And the next.

Jonno slouched at the baseline as his father rained more balls at him for serving. When he was old enough and strong enough, he would one day drill some aces past his father. But right now there was no way to "show him" anything—except that he, Jonno, didn't have to try to please him. Without a word, he walked slowly to the gate, off the court, and across the grass to the drinking fountain.

The water, briefly, was warm and gritty, but soon cooled to a breath from an underground spring. He drank deeply and held his head in the stream until his father spoke behind him.

"What's going on, Jonno? As soon as you hit something that doesn't come easily, you give up?"

He couldn't tell his father that he might hate him. So he yelled, "I hate tennis!" knowing full well that tennis was not the problem. "It's a dumb, stupid sport full of lines you can't cross and words that don't make sense."

It was one of the few times he had seen his father look confused. "Then why did you come?"

"Because you told me we were coming."

"But you never said you didn't want to!" His father's face was turning deeper red under the sweat. "Damn it, Jonno! You're doing it again! You never tell me what you're thinking!"

"Maybe that's because you never listen! Because I know you only care what you're thinking!" The words came welling up like drinking-fountain water, and he seemed to be too tired to turn them off. "Rob listens to me, though. He understands! He even understands what I don't say!"

His father looked thunderstruck.

Kate and Peter were coming, galloping across the field in a giddy game of keep-away.

"I wiped her out," Peter yelled. "Total game score: thirty-three to love."

"My talents lie elsewhere!" Kate did a jazzy sashay to a

snatch of *Porgy and Bess* their mother loved. " 'Oh, I got plenty of nuthin'.' " She strummed her racket like a guitar. " 'And nuthin's plenty for me.' "

Jonno bolted for the car. Kate and that songwriter had the words just right, but not the meaning. There was nothing left of his morning's hope, and plenty of nothing to look forward to.

"Haarrhhh! Haarrhhh! Haarrhhh! Welcome back, sports fans, from me and my colleague, Whizzer Whooper, making a third try at completing our broadcast of this crucial game."

Where the wings of Gram's house met and sheltered the weathered cedar deck, Jonno straddled a deck chair, scrunched over his gameboard, and tried to forget his troubles. The first trouble was this third day of bleak weather—too cool for swimming, too rough for sailing. The second was that he had walked the ocean beach and cove at all times of daylight over the past two days without a glimpse of Rob Loud.

The family was coexisting in a state of uneasy truce. "Have you seen the piper anymore?" Alison kept asking. And roaming the beach with his father, Pip, and Alison, Jonno sensed that his father was as alert as he for Rob's next appearance. "Looks as if your friend has left town," Phil Ayres remarked too casually as they left the cove behind.

Reading relief and satisfaction in his father's words, Jonno had to bite back a bitter reply. But he was stung hard enough to confront his father with a question. "What if he were here, Dad? You said you were going to make inquiries."

Unexpectedly, his father didn't have the right words ready. He stopped scuffing along the sandy track and turned a searching look on Jonno. More unexpectedly, the look softened as he laid a hand on Jonno's shoulder. Still, all he said was, "We'll see. I'd like to meet the man myself."

But there had been no glimpse, no sound. Certainly, no ringing up. So now Jonno sat under a pewter sky, and felt vaguely and unreasonably grouchy. The house was quiet, since Kate and Alison had gone to town with Dad. Behind him on the roofpeak, Gram's goose wavered in an uncertain breeze. The day was neither here nor there. He wished just anything would happen.

"Haarrhhh! Haarrhhh! I can't remember a time when these two rivals have had this much trouble finishing nine innings of baseball. How about you, Whizzer? No, sports fans, Whizzer can't either."

His mother slid back the deck door, humming something full of *alleluias* and carrying a half-knitted sweater. Jonno watched as she plunked herself tailor-fashion on a cushion and realized she was staring at him instead of her yarn tangle.

"Jonathan Ayres," she declared, "you haven't been so itchy since the first day of first grade, when you told me all you'd done all day was sit at a desk and sweat."

Jonno shrugged. *"Haarrhhh! Haarrhhh!* You may recall, sports fans, the game was called the other day because of sandstorms; it's the eighth meeting of the season for these two teams. . . . Eighth—Mom, what's an octave?"

"An eight-note interval in music. C to C, G to G," she mumbled into her knitting. "What in the world made you think of that?"

"Just something I read." He was having a lot of trouble today caring about the Yankees and the Red Sox. "There's been a lot of wild surmise about what this series will do to the season standings, and Whizzer and I will give you a full analysis as the game goes on. . . . Mom, what's a tartan?"

His mother put down her knitting and looked at him quizzically. "It's a special plaid worn by a clan in Scotland, sort of a family uniform. They still wear tartan kilts for ceremonial occasions, pipers and all. Ahh. That piper really did get to you, didn't he?"

To Jonno's relief, the phone rang in the kitchen beyond the sliding door. Gram's determined footsteps sounded on the stairs, but Jess Ayres was up and through the door in one swift motion, and back almost as quickly, after a few brief murmurs in a tone of some surprise.

"You don't mean it!" Behind her, Gram let out a squawk of indignation.

"Haarrhhh!" More questions, thought Jonno, or a lecture to make my day complete.

Instead, his mother ruffled his hair playfully. "Take heart, Jonathan Ayres! What a wonderful accent he has, your friend Mr. Loud. That was he, saying he'd like to come by to see if you'd want a walk with him."

Jonno kept his gaze on the dice he hadn't tossed yet. "And what did you tell him?"

His mother made an easy gesture with her hands. "I said to come along, that I would like to meet him." She lowered her voice. "Gram has her own view on the matter, but I thought he sounded very nice."

I tried to tell you that, thought Jonno, but his funk was

lifting. As the grumpiness drained out of him, he felt light all over. He wanted to shout and jump up and down like Alison, but instead he made an efficient show of stashing away the baseball game and score sheets. By the time he took them inside, his mother had combed her hair and his grandmother was teetering on tiptoe on the stair landing, trying to close the porthole window.

With a final triumphant swat, Gram turned and bustled down the stairs. "Thank the Lord it's a cool day and we won't suffocate with the windows shut!" she exclaimed. "If he's bringing that infernal instrument with him it'll raise our roof, but a least we can spare the neighbors!"

Jonno thought for the hundredth time that the Lord was probably concerned with more serious problems, but just in case he offered a speedy little prayer of his own that Gram would restrain herself when Rob arrived. From the way she settled herself in the corner rocker with an air of preparing for battle, things looked ominous. Pip, always wary of extraordinary bustle, had flattened himself on the floor and he looked worried, too. Jonno bent over him as another precaution. "Just do me a favor, Pip," he whispered. "Pretend you love bagpipes."

His mother's mood was more of a mystery. She seemed edgy as she scooped Monopoly pieces from the floor in front of the fireplace, but Jonno thought she stifled a giggle when she glanced at Gram, on guard in her corner. When the knock came on Gram's Dutch door, she moved to it quickly.

"Good day," Rob rumbled cheerily. "I'm Rob Loud, and ye're Jonno's mother, I can tell."

"Do come in, Mr. Loud. I'm Jess Ayres and here's Jonathan, glad to see you."

"Hello there, Jonno." Rob shook the hand Jess Ayres offered and looked past Jonno to the corner where Gram sat glaring at the pipes resting in the crook of his left arm. "And good day to you, ma'am," he called cheerily.

"How do you do," said Gram icily.

"Another Mrs. Ayres, you must be—Jonno's Gram," Rob went on, undaunted. "And is it you that grows those geraniums and the glorious garden by the gate? I do like a garden with a wildflower look to it."

Gram began to look less starchy.

"I've had good luck, myself, with geraniums by the sea," Rob declared. "And it's a wonder, isn't it, what salt air does for hollyhocks?"

It was the first time Jonno had ever seen Gram at a loss for words. When she thought of something to say, she sounded incredulous. "Do you garden, Mr. Loud?" It was the same tone she would have used if Mrs. Goodspeed had told her she had taken up hang gliding.

Rob heard it, too, for he threw Jonno a mirthful, side-long look before he answered. "Aye, that I do. Just a wee patch I keep now, but bonnie." He turned back to Jonno's mother. "Your son's good company for a solitary old wanderer like me, and I'm glad to have a chance to tell you how fine a lad I find him. 'Twas me, you know, made him late the other evenin'."

"Humph," said Gram loudly.

But Jess Ayres watched Rob intently, and Jonno thought a smile was growing in her clear brown eyes. Maybe it was going to be all right after all. His mother knew a nice person when she met one.

"Will you walk a while then, Jonno?" Rob went on.

"Is it okay, Mom?"

His mother nodded. "Just don't forget the hour, this time."

So, neatly and even diplomatically, Rob had him headed up the lane before you could say Grace Goodspeed. Jonno chuckled. Such finesse was unexpected.

"What's so funny, Jonathan Ayres?"

"Not funny—great! Everything!" Jonno loped along sideways and looked into the man's face. "I didn't think you'd really call. And I guess I'm laughing at how you melted Gram. Her flowers were the best thing to talk about, if you wanted to get her mind off Mrs. Goodspeed."

"Hmm. It wasn't just talk, y'know, about the garden; it's like a summer meadow. And she's still hostile, yer gram, though she did thaw slightly. It seems she just has better taste in flowers than in friends," said Rob drily. "But about the callin', Jonno—when I tell you something, you can believe it."

"I didn't exactly disbelieve you. I guess I just thought you might decide it was too much trouble."

"Oh, no. I'd have rung you sooner, but John Farnum dragged me off to Boston for a couple of days. We just got back this mornin'." Rob stopped for a moment and took a deep breath. "I need to clear out the cobwebs. I never was a great one for cities."

"Rob, where are your flowers? Your patch, that you told Gram about?"

"In the dooryard of my parents' cottage, which is mine

now, in a wee crossroads of a place called Cloudoon, on the other edge of your ocean."

Even Rob's facts sounded like a story.

"What did your father do there?" Jonno asked.

"Fished. And farmed. And kept sheep. It's a place where a body must use all his skills just to make a livin'. Let's stop a bit," Rob said as they passed through the hedgerows onto the bluff. "My leg's weary from bein' poked by over-enthusiastic medicine men, and I've somethin' for you, anyway."

Rob sank down on the splintery bench that overlooked the gray expanse of sea and inlet, and fumbled in the knap-sack slung over his left shoulder. "I don't have a goose," he said oddly, "but here's a practice chanter y'might try." He drew a slender pipe from the pouch over his shoulder and handed it to Jonno. "Take it, lad! It won't bite!"

Rob was full of surprises today. Jonno thought he had made it clear that music was not his thing. Yet it wasn't just politeness that made him stretch out both hands. The prac-tice chanter wasn't too forbidding—more like recorders he'd been made to try at school than the mass of pipes on Rob's left arm.

"Now, if you were learnin' to play the pipes," Rob said, "you'd start on this to learn fingerin' and breathin'. Then you'd try the goose, a small bag with a blowpipe and chanter, before goin' on to the big pipes. Have a go, why don't ye, just to get the feel of it. Put your hands so, and try any note. Just a little blow."

Jonno put the slender pipe in his mouth and blew tim-idly. The chanter gave a choked, flat bleat.

"Harder, with a better breath," said Rob.

Maybe, if he made a horrible enough noise, Rob would give up on him. Jonno took a breath big enough for the biggest baritone in his mother's choir, and blew mightily. The chanter squealed in protest. But Rob only chuckled.

"Ye can't overblow, either. Remember ye need a nice, steady flow of air."

"But if it has to be steady," protested Jonno, "when do you ever get to breathe?"

"When ye breathe, with the big pipes, ye pump the bag with yer elbow to keep the air flowin'. For instance, here's the basic scale: G, A, B, C, D, E, F, G, A." Rob played it effortlessly, his shoulders thrown back, his right leg thrust out awkwardly before him. "If ye want to try it—behind a solid door, so's not to fluster yer gram—I'll write it out for you later."

What he really wanted was to talk, but Rob looked so enthusiastic that Jonno hadn't the heart to interrupt him.

"Jonathan Ayres." The lines around the gray eyes deepened, and the corners of Rob's mouth lifted. "Would ye like to hold my pipes then, just to see what it feels like?"

That might be a once-in-a-lifetime offer. Jonno nodded.

"Set down the chanter then, and stand." Rob laid the long pipes on Jonno's left shoulder, tucked the bag under his arm and helped him wrap his hands around the chanter. The blowpipe wavered under Jonno's nose, and the whole arrangement felt very insecure. Surely a person needed more than two hands to control this monster!

Rob lifted the pipes away, smiling gently at Jonno's mild panic. "Y'see why a beginnin' piper goes one step at a time."

Jonno was beginning to feel caught up in a current.

"Rob, even if I wanted to play the pipes, maybe I'm already to old to learn. I don't even know if anyone in America could teach me."

Rob was as persistent as Dad with his tennis. "Horsefeathers, lad! Y're never too old to try something that's important to you! As for teachers, there must be good ones—in the games at Cowal two years past, I saw a young Yank win the piping competition!"

Half of Jonno's mind registered Rob's pep talk about piping, but the other half had fixed on the feeling that this was uncomfortably like one of his father's more subtle persuasions. "Rob," he said, "there's something I need to ask you."

Rob's eyes acknowledged the urgency in Jonno's voice, but even so his right forefinger slashed the space between them, driving his own point home. "I just want to tell ye, Jonno, if ye want something enough, there's always a way!" Rob cocked his head quizzically and looked more gentle. "Now, what's yer question?"

Jonno sat down beside Rob, turning the practice chanter in his hands. "I know this will sound funny," he said, "but did you really like your father?"

"Ah. 'Like,' as opposed to 'love' or 'respect'?"

Jonno nodded. He was leaning forward with his elbows on his knees, staring toward the sea, but Rob was quiet such a while that Jonno turned back to see if he was going to answer.

"Not funny, Jonno. A good question." Rob shifted on the bench and winced a little. "At first, I didn't get much chance to find out if I liked my da—he worked all the time, and I did what bairns do and hardly saw him. When I was old enough, I worked with him, but he wasn't a great talker. So I thought of him as someone older, distant—someone almost from a different time, or a different planet. I loved him. I respected him. But I kept my own counsel, too. And I didn't appreciate him, really, till 'twas nearly too late. Only then I found that in order to know him, and like him, I had to meet him halfway."

Jonno shook his head. It sounded like a puzzle. "Halfway?"

"Jonno." Rob laid his free hand on Jonno's shoulder. "I'm just sayin', if y' want to like yer da more, y' may have to try to talk to him the way ye talk to me."

Jonno sighed. "He doesn't listen."

"Well," said Rob quietly, "think whether ye must give him more to listen to." His fist thumped Jonno's shoulder lightly. "Let's walk along the bluff a way; my leg feels stiff again."

Jonno stood up and stretched. Above the sea, lowering clouds threatened to blot out the horizon. He watched a flock of geese fly low across the inlet, half-aware that Rob was pulling his leg in gingerly, starting to stand.

Suddenly Rob sat back with a thud and drove his fist sideways against the back of the bench. "Damn it to hell!" he muttered, as breathlessly as if he'd just run a hundred-yard dash. He threw back his head, drew a breath that made his chest heave, and exhaled in a quiet flood of curses that surpassed anything Jonno had heard when his father packed the car. All the four-letter words Jonno had learned in fourth grade, Rob peppered and punctuated with English words that made no sense and furious foreign words that must be Gaelic. It was virtuoso cursing, and

Jonno was lost admiring it until he realized Rob's face looked ashen beneath the tan.

Rob shook his head. "I'm sorry, lad, it's the blasted leg; it just gives out now and again."

"But what did the doctors say? The ones who just looked at it."

Rob waved his hand impatiently. "They advocated some institutional hocus-pocus that I want no part of. Come on, Jonno, I'd best get back to the Farnums'."

"I can carry the knapsack. Even the pipes—I'll be really careful," Jonno offered quickly, but Rob shook his head again.

"I'm so used to the pipes they're like part of myself, but ye could take this." He passed Jonno the knapsack, which was unexpectedly heavy. "I've some books in there that don't make it any lighter."

Jonno tucked the practice chanter in the knapsack and slung it over his right shoulder. At half the speed of their coming, they moved off the edge of the bluff, Rob first leaning on Jonno, gradually letting his leg bear more weight but taking sharp, snatching breaths each time he stepped on it. There was no more swearing. Rob stopped talking, as if every fiber of mind and body was needed to propel him along the dirt road that led to the Farnums'.

"Ye've a good strong back, Jonno," Rob finally managed as they started up the long rise to the Farnums' porch. "Don't worry, lad. I'm just takin' care not to land in a blitherin', blasphemin' heap. It's no calamity, this. It happens all the time."

All the time! For all the years since whatever happened in that war? Why would he live with this if there was a remedy, this man full of stories to set a person dreaming, this man who'd told him about wild surmise?

"But Rob, can't somebody help? Don't doctors know more now than they did when you got hurt?"

Rob took another sucking breath and let it out in a puff of impatience. "So they say." He stood still. "But I've too much regard for the spirit in me, Jonno, to let this get the best of me. I'm damned if I'll let 'em shut me up in a hospital with tubes runnin' in and out, all in the name of progress."

"But," Jonno blurted without trying to be tactful, "what if it gets worse?"

Rob turned up the rise again. "I've lived with the thing this long—it's like an old messmate: aggravatin' but predictable." He pounded Jonno's shoulder in a way that seemed playful, but his jaw was set and his voice still strained. "I'm too old to go lookin' for a new devil. I'll keep the one I know, thanks."

It seemed that Rob was talking to himself as much as to Jonno, deciding something important and final. Maybe, deciding wrong. For what he was saying now contradicted everything he'd said before, about finding ways, about endless possibilities. "Too old to go lookin' for a new devil," he now declared about himself.

Rob was no hypocrite, spouting principles he wouldn't follow. Rather, he seemed—Jonno's mind hovered around the word—afraid. Of tubes, as he'd said, of hospital walls, and all the eerie machines of modern medicine. Afraid of losing his freedom.

Well, Jonno was afraid for different reasons. Not of

what doctors might do to Rob, but of what might happen to him without them. Crippled, he'd be free no longer.

Words came welling up unbidden, as they had the other day with his father. With Rob, he needn't try to hold them back. So, twisting to look into Rob's face, grasping Rob's arm, he cried, "You can't say you're too old! You just finished telling me it's never too late to try something important!"

Rob's face flushed deep red with anger. "That's enough, Jonno!" He snatched his arm away from Jonno's shoulder and threw off Jonno's anxious hand, straightening with another swift breath. "Don't preach at me, laddie. I don't need to hear my own words thrown back at me."

Jonno put out a hand to help again, but Rob brushed him away. "Ye're drivin' me crazy," he said gruffly. "Leave me be. I can make it on my own."

Jonno watched him labor up the path to the Farnums' porch. Mrs. Farnum must have seen him coming, for she met him at the door with a sympathetic murmur and gave Jonno a friendly wave as they disappeared inside.

Jonno felt as if he had been hit in the stomach with a pitched ball. How long he stood stunned, he wasn't sure. He only knew his eyes stung ominously and he had to get away.

He turned to run and Rob's knapsack thumped against his shoulder, so he sprinted up the path and flung it in a great arc toward the porch, wanting just to be rid of it and gone. Only when he was off down the knoll and the knapsack had hit the porch with a thunk did he remember that it held the practice chanter.

Words of Rob's dogged him as he ran.

"Jonno, when I tell you somethin', you can believe it. . . . Ye're drivin' me crazy. . . . I can make it on my own."

The worst of it was that he felt betrayed. He had only said what he felt without considering the consequences, just as when he'd played the piper's clansman, the other morning on the beach. But today Rob, who had always understood everything, understood nothing. It would feel good right now to be five years old, able to sit down in a sandy rut and cry.

Jonno plunged into Gram's lane, realizing vaguely that he had crossed the main road without even pausing to check for traffic. His eyes still stung. His breath rasped in his throat. Worst of all was the sick, leaden feeling in the place Coach Kluck called the solar plexus. Why did people say their hearts were heavy, when it really felt more like your stomach?

Beyond the jog in the lane just ahead, Alison's family of quail startled up as he came nearer. Before the whir of wings subsided, Jonno pulled himself back to a scuffling walk. Why was he in such a rush that he had to frighten a bunch of harmless birds? He didn't understand what had made Rob so angry, but angry he was. So there was no need to run anymore, nothing worth running to. No point in chasing voices on the wind.

The station wagon in Gram's driveway meant that Dad, Kate, and Alison were back from town. He wouldn't face Al's bubbly curiosity if he could help it. Nor Kate's latest quotations from Peter the Wonderful. Most of all, he wouldn't face his father's quick eyes and probing questions. So he slipped through the shrubs on the near side of the house and peered at the deck, around the ivy-hung trunk of a pine tree.

The pulse of Kate's music vibrated under the eaves.

Gram must have decided she was suffocating after all, for the sound of voices drifted through some open windows, but no one was in sight. He could safely settle on the flat rock by the stairs and keep his thoughts to himself until some of the sting went out of them.

Jonno bent forward from the waist and circled the deck in a silent shuffle. The rock was a chilly refuge with no sun to warm it, but at least he was out of sight and below the reach of the breeze that still fitfully spun the goose on Gram's roof. Jonno sank onto the rock gratefully, arms around his knees, head bent over them. He'd like to roll himself up in a ball, like a hedgehog warding off intruders.

Two ants played tag on the ragged toe of Jonno's left sneaker. At the edge of the yard a brown rabbit, encouraged by his stillness, hopped briskly toward the neighbor's garden. The damp breeze breathed through the tree over Jonno's head. Inside the house, his mother's laugh rippled. I'd be sleepy, he thought, if I weren't beginning to feel cold.

"I thought he was pretty charming myself!" All at once, his mother's voice came very clearly through the kitchen window.

Jonno didn't move a muscle, but his sleepiness fled. She must be standing at the sink starting supper, and she might be talking about Rob Loud.

"He's really rather dashing and at the same time—oh, a little wistful," she went on. "I can see why he's captivated Jonno. Especially with that bagpipe."

Dad must be right at her elbow. "It seems he's a lot more than dashing. I'd only met Colonel Farnum once before, you know, and he's pretty reserved—Grace

Goodspeed probably has her troubles with him, too. But when I ran into him at the store, he was downright talkative. He actually hailed me to tell me how much his friend likes Jonno. It's interesting, because I gather Loud's something of a loner and has no family of his own."

"Well, he seems to have plenty to say to Jonno," Mom replied. "You should have seen them going up that lane— he had Jonno beaming, waving his arms, and talking a mile a minute."

There seemed to be a long pause before Phil Ayres spoke again. "You know, Jess," he said astonishingly, "I kind of envy the man. It sounds as if he's touched some depths in Jonno that I can only guess about. I wonder how he's managed that so quickly."

Water ran in the sink. "If they're both kind of quiet," said Jonno's mother rather carefully, "maybe he's a good listener. Or maybe," she added more lightly, "they're just plain kindred spirits. But," she prompted, "you said, 'a lot more than dashing.' For goodness sake," her voice receded as she moved around the kitchen and came back, "tell me more!"

Silently and fervently, Jonno agreed. That his father might be really troubled about not knowing him better was a new idea, startling and unbelievable. But it was the part about Rob that made him strain back against the deck pilings, trying to catch every word, though every word his father said weighed heavier on his growing sense of loss.

"They met somewhere in France or Belgium during World War II, sometime after D-Day," Phil Ayres said. "John Farnum was so aboil with stories that I'm a bit muddled; I'm not sure whether they were in a hospital or a prisoner-of-war camp, but the gist of it was that Loud had piped some commandos ashore in Normandy and fought through a lot of France with them before he was finally wounded. Then his leg was broken by shrapnel and has never healed quite right, which John says was a common problem. Without all the antibiotics we have now, a lot of people developed chronic infections from wounds like that."

"But now, surely . . ." Jess Ayres began.

"The Farnums are trying to convince him to go into a hospital for treatment, but he's evidently as mulish as he is intriguing, and highly allergic to confinement. Anyway . . ." His father's voice rose with his familiar story-teller's relish. "Colonel Farnum knew a Britisher who told him an absolutely hair-raising tale about seeing Loud parading up and down the invasion beach, with his pipes wailing through machine gun and mortar fire. Playing some song about flowers!"

Not flowers, thought Jonno. Scottish soldiers on the move. Bluebonnets.

"And John Farnum said when the two of them were together, it was Loud who really kept him going."

Jonno could imagine. "And here's a hand, my trusty friend," said Rob's voice in his memory.

"Then," Phil Ayres's voice grew louder as he slid back the deck door and peered out at the overcast sky, "he talked about a paratrooper who'd been dropped in the night behind the assault beaches. This fellow told John about capturing a bridge, waiting and waiting for the landing forces to catch up with them, and hearing first, through all the firing, the skirl of Loud's pipes. Just like the cavalry bugles in the old Westerns!"

Jonno could imagine that, too. From crouching on a foggy dune and kneeling in a sunny hollow, he knew how the sound of pipes could twist the heart, or lift it.

Footsteps sounded on the deck and suddenly Phil Ayres stood over Jonno's head. "Jonno, you gave me a start! We didn't know you were back. Don't you want to come inside? I might even build a fire—it's getting raw out here."

Jonno gripped his knees tighter and wished again for a hedgehog's spines. "I haven't been here long, Dad," he said. "I'll be in soon."

"Did you hear what I was telling Mom? I ran into Colonel Farnum in the village, and he says your friend Mr. Loud was quite a hero."

Jonno's mind spun like the goose on the rooftop. Quite a hero. It would have been nice if they could have just taken his word that Rob was an all-right person. Instead, here was his father weaving another saga, turning Rob into another of his personal treasures.

"Jonno, is something wrong?"

Jonno shook his head, but his father stood his ground.

"Why don't you come up here and tell me what's bothering you?"

Reluctantly, stiffly, Jonno uncoiled and swung himself onto the deck. He shrugged. "Mr. Loud's leg was bothering him so he went back to the Farnums' and sent me home."

"Was he unpleasant about it? You seem upset."

Again, the pang in the solar plexus. "I felt kind of told to get lost."

Jonno's father looked at him long enough to make Jonno wonder what was going on behind the hazel eyes. "One possibility you ought to consider," Phil Ayres said finally, "is that Mr. Loud's being gruff with you doesn't mean he was angry at you. He could be angry at himself, at life, at chronic pain. Lord knows you've heard me explode at times when what was really bothering me was a conniving colleague or an overload of work, and you just happened to cross my path at the wrong moment."

Jonno remembered countless times: when he'd dropped the huge, unabridged dictionary and been told, "Stay out of my study when I'm trying to work!"; when a burst bicycle tire had been dismissed with a curt, "That is just not a high-priority problem—Jonno, you're driving me crazy!"

"I'd like to think I've always apologized," his father went on, "but life being as hectic as it is, I probably haven't."

"You mean, you didn't mean what you said, sometimes, and maybe Rob didn't either?"

"Sure. A lot of rotten things said in anger are almost like a cry for understanding. Listen to a couple of little kids fighting some day. Or listen to yourself and Kate—you haven't declared a truce yet."

"But it's hard to be understanding when you're a kid and the angry person is a grown-up who's yelling at you."

The breeze in the pines seemed louder as his father hesitated. "Yes," said Phil Ayres quietly. "I tend to forget that."

The slider's rumble behind him was followed by his mother's step on the deck and her arms around Jonno's neck. "What's interesting enough to keep you two out here in the damp?"

"Oh," said her husband lightly, "I found Jonno out here in a huddle and kept him cornered for a little private conversation."

The slider swooshed again. So much for privacy, Jonno thought resignedly.

"I beat Gram in Chinese checkers!" cried Alison.

"It was scarcely a contest!" Gram exclaimed. "That child has the soul of a riverboat gambler! My stars, it's dank out here! Jonno, you'll catch your death of cold." Her voice grew sharper. "You've been out a long while. How was your walk?"

"Okay," said Jonno, stretching and turning toward the house.

"Is that all!" Gram snorted. "I expected an adventure story, after all these Rob Loud legends your father brought home. It's amazing how a couple of tall tales can sweep you off your feet, Philip Ayres."

"Or maybe, Mother, my mind's been changed by facts," said Jonno's father.

Peppering, Gram stared at Jonno and then glared up at her son. "Or maybe by the look of him Jonno's changing his mind about his piper."

Jonno stiffened with his hand on the doorframe.

"Why, Jonno, why?" asked Alison. "Did something bad happen?"

"No!" All the afternoon's frustration was boiling over, and Jonno turned on Alison. "Damn it, Alison, leave me alone!"

Alison turned white, and Jonno was nearly as shocked

as she was. He had never talked to her that way before.

"Jonno, watch your language," said his mother sharply.

Gram looked disgusted and Dad, reaching for Alison's shoulder, looked ominous, but the tension was broken by the screechy raising of Kate's dormer window.

"Ohh!" Kate's head appeared, looking more frazzled and drowsy than usual. "Why don't you leave the poor kid alone?"

"Buzz off, Kate," said Jonno tersely, surprising himself again, before he realized that he wasn't sure which "poor kid" she'd been defending.

Kate propped her elbow on the sill and her chin on her fist so hard that her curls bounced. "Why can't anyone leave anyone alone around here?" she demanded dramatically. "A person can't even take a nap in peace!"

"Your woofers have been making more noise than anything," Jonno said calmly. "You're a great one to talk about peace and leaving people alone."

"This does appear to be a clear case of the pot calling the kettle black," Jess Ayres chuckled.

"You'd better watch it, Kate," their father added. "You might get mellow in your old age. Come on down and we'll build a fire. I think what we've got here is an epidemic of cabin fever."

Gram shivered and followed his parents indoors, but Alison hung back. Her eyes were still reproachful. Seeing her hurt, Jonno understood how someone could explode unfairly. He had just done the same thing to her that Rob had done to him. At least, with her, he could make peace.

"Al," he said, "I'm sorry."

But with Rob the next move was out of his hands.

Maybe he wasn't ready for such a complicated friendship. It seemed that wild surmise could hurt too much. He had better stick with friends like Doug and Mickey, whose most unpredictable qualities were their taste in new sneakers, or the number of days they wore the same pair of socks.

A stronger wind sighed across the roof and through the pines. Off in a thicket a quail called softly. Jonno looked up and saw that Gram's goose was heading resolutely toward the harbor. The sea wind had steadied from the northeast. He shivered and shoved back the sliding door. He was cold all the way to his bones.

"Pip! Pippin!" Jonno whistled and stalked onto the deck like an Indian scout, listening intently, but there was no encouraging jingle of dog tags to tell him Pip was bumbling back through someone's shrubbery. "Hey, Pippi-in."

Drat the dog. Drat the day. Drat his father's notion to tour historic sites with a northeaster brewing. Jonno had been grateful to settle for a book and Pip's company. They had left him with a picnic lunch and a lot of admonitions. "Check all the windows if the rain starts. Take Pip for a run, but stay close to home. Stay off the beach."

So double-drat the dog. Jonno had been depressed enough since yesterday, without Pip's causing trouble, too. It didn't help now to realize that he should have paid attention to the wild barking on the deck a while ago. It had felt so good to be lost in a story, dealing with someone else's hopes and scares and disappointments instead of his own, that he'd just been glad when Pip quieted down and he could roll over on the couch to finish the chapter.

Well, Pippin hadn't just quieted down. He had disappeared. If he'd been in a fight, Jonno would have heard it. More likely he had run off after a rabbit or some quail. Neither quick enough to catch a rabbit nor crafty enough to surprise the quail, he just seemed to relish the chase. The strange thing was that he'd normally be back by now, panting and sheepish. After all, a retriever's business was supposed to be bringing things home, himself included.

Hopefully, Jonno whistled again. "Pippin!"

Nothing.

Gram's goose still pointed steadily inland, and clouds scudded low overhead, running from the sea. It seemed the weather had worsened just in the five minutes he'd been out here hooting and hollering. If he was going after Pip, he had better be about it.

A litany of family cautions sounded in his head. "Check all the windows if the rain starts." Jonno spun back through the deck door, slid it shut and locked it securely, then sped from room to room latching windows. The porthole. The loft. Out through the breezeway, doors slamming, up and down the ladderlike stairs like a seaman called to battle station. "Latch the garage door. Lock the back door. Don't forget the house key." He snatched the key on the long leather thong from its hook in the kitchen and slid it over his head like a necklace.

"Stay close to home." Right now, that seemed to be up to Pip. Jonno shot a few of Rob Loud's clearer curses at the snarled laces of his sneakers. "Stay off the beach." Who knew where he would have to go? Was it better to leave Pip out in the weather or to disobey? At least, he'd better leave a note in the usual place, speared on the fishhook that hung on the wall of the breezeway.

"Mom and Dad—Pip took off after something and hasn't come back. Gone to find him. Back soon. Jonno."

Hoping that sounded reassuring and responsible, Jonno forced his scribble onto the hook and folded its bottom under a shingle to keep it from flapping in the wind. Then he charged back through the house, checked the latch on the front door and raced out into the lane, yelling as he ran. "Pip! Pippin, you dumb dog, come here!"

With the wind at his back, Jonno headed for the harbor end of the lane; Pip might have followed someone to the town landing. But there he found only wading shore birds and idle fishing boats anchored in the narrow channel left at low tide. The people who made their living on these waters knew when it was a day to stay on dry land.

"Pippin!" Jonno turned back up the lane toward the bluff, his head bent into the wind, swinging to and fro like Gram's weather vane, to holler in one direction and then another. His anxiety was giving way to anger. Where was that crazy dog, anyway? Especially with the tide out, he could have sloshed his way almost anywhere.

If someone had told Jonno yesterday that things could be even worse, he would have thought that a bad joke. The void cut by Rob's parting words still ached deep inside him. And in it churned a sickening mixture of anger at Pip and apprehension about his parents' reaction to his taking off for points unknown. It might be a relief to leave here this year, he thought with dismay. Finding and losing Rob, letting go of Peter, this vacation had gotten beyond the comfortable bounds of fun and exercise and routinely teasing sisters.

Jonno charged down the tangled corridor of bushes that ended on the bluff, hoarse and lightheaded from running and yelling. The wind bit hard as soon as he cleared the hedges, knifing through the holes in his slouchy sweatshirt and slapping its folds against his sides as if it were a flag snapping on a pole.

He stared off the bluff at a gray world. Fog had already swallowed the ocean; now it licked the dunes on the outer beach and the farthest reaches of the inlet. Gray sky, gray water. Gray spirit. Much as Pip would, Jonno shook himself in the wind. He forced out a flurry of whistles and a barrage of bellows that he thought might finish his voice. And that was when he heard the barking.

Was that Pip, that shadowy shape way out on the sandbar, curiously anchored by some object in the sand? As Jonno watched, the animal flipflopped from side to side, then scrambled to a crouch, right side up but caught and dejected.

"Pippin!" Jonno yelled again, and the figure came to a semblance of Pip's attention, its head twisted hopefully toward his voice.

Impressions flashed in Jonno's mind like slides on a screen aglare with light. It was Pip. And if his paw was caught, he was stuck on the sandbar until someone could free him. The tide would turn soon. It would come in fast and hard before the storm. And at high tide, that sandbar was quite invisible. Before dark, the spot where Pip struggled would be three feet under water.

Anger, cold, and sadness fled. Jonno hurtled down the forty-two steps, leaping the last three, rushing to reach the boats beached in the cove.

If only he had Gram's familiar rowboat, which was back at the landing. Just hauling a boat into the water at low tide would take some doing for a boy alone, and then there'd be at least a couple of hundred yards to row, so he had to find something light and maneuverable. On a nice, calm day he'd have zipped out on a sunfish and let Pip swim back. No hope of that today, beating against the wind; he'd capsize in a minute, and then who would rescue him?

"Stay away from the beach" echoed on the fringes of his mind, but Jonno knew his father would be the first one out after any creature in distress. "You must never get into a boat without the owner's permission"—that was harder to dismiss. But there was no time, maybe just minutes more of slack tide! And wasn't there an ancient law of the sea about never ignoring an SOS?

Just below the high-water line on the inner slope of the cove was a battered little skiff that looked familiar. Jonno had seen it bobbing at anchor enough times to know that it was seaworthy. On his knees in cold ooze, Jonno dug out the anchor and tossed it into the boat. Oars, yes. Wreathing the bow line around his shoulders and grasping it with both hands behind his back, he strained toward the water, tugging and resting, until at last he could run around to the stern and shove it the last few yards from behind.

"Hold on, Pip! I'm comin'!" he yelled in the direction of the mist-hung sandbar. A faint bark seemed to answer, but Jonno was too busy getting himself afloat to be certain. His sneakers got soaked in the process, but he might as well keep them on; it wasn't as if things were going to get any drier. He set the stubby oars in their locks and tried to steady the skiff on a straight line to the sandbar.

The water was choppy, and he had to work hard to make headway. He pulled on the oars and wondered what his father would say about his setting out alone in such weather. Mom and Gram would be horrified, Mom because of the danger and Gram because of the broken rules. Alison would wish she had been here. "Demented,"

Kate would say, unless Peter intervened. And Peter? Jonno grinned. In the face of any physical challenge, Peter always said the same thing: "Go for it."

Well, the truth was he'd rather not be going for it. But even in the mist, glances over his shoulder told him that the sandbar was getting closer.

The skiff ran aground with a jolt. His shoulders burned, his arms ached and his hands hurt, but Pip's joyful barking made Jonno feel more confident. Surely if the dog were really hurt he wouldn't be making so much noise. Jonno shipped the oars and hopped out onto the oozing rim of the sandbar. He dug in his heels and hauled on the skiff's bow until his burning muscles screamed. Dad would have beached it higher, but this would have to do. He threw out the anchor and slogged toward Pip as fast as the mire allowed. He soon saw that one of Pip's front paws was caught inside the half-buried ruin of a lobster pot.

Jonno could guess what had happened. Pip had paddled out to the sandbar as he often did. Then off he'd raced after a flock of gulls or a flight of terns, watching his quarry instead of his feet, and so he'd blundered into a trap uncovered by the last strong tide.

"It's okay, Pip, you crazy ol' dog," Jonno cried as he ran the last few yards and dropped to his knees to assess Pip's problem.

Jonno hoped it was okay. The wall of fog loomed closer, and he was beginning to feel cold in spite of exertion. Pip whimpered and wiggled and licked Jonno's comforting hands, but though his tail swished a crescent in the wet sand, he looked exhausted. It'll be a wonder if that leg's not broken, Jonno thought.

Pip's paw had struck the trap at just the right angle to slip between the wooden slats, and he'd worked it in deeper trying to get away. Would those old slats flex enough to free him? Wondering, Jonno moved around the buried lobster pot to face Pip, knelt down, and threw all his weight forward, one hand pressing down on the slat behind Pip's paw, the other hand pulling upward on the slat in front of it. Pip twisted the trapped leg with a pitiful whimper, but the gap Jonno forced was still too narrow.

The slats could be broken by jumping on the pot, but that might hurt Pip's leg more than what had happened already. Jonno wished fervently for the crowbar propped in the corner of Gram's garage, but there was no time to go ashore for tools. The fog was still coming, a frantic glance told him. The tide would soon be coming, too.

Whatever he could do must be done with his own hands. And feet. And quickly. Maybe an oar! Jonno jumped to Pippin's side and threw his arms around the big, shaggy neck. "Don't worry, Pip; I'll be right back." Pip licked his face. Then Jonno was up and off again to fetch an oar.

Already water lapped under the skiff's stern. The tide was moving in. Now every minute lost meant a longer pull to shore.

The blade of the oar slid easily between the slats of the lobster pot, but the handle, too thick, resisted. Standing beside Pip, Jonno stopped shoving with a flash of apprehension. Could the oar be snapped in two by the pressure? For that matter, could the oar be caught like Pippin's paw? Then they'd both be trapped on the sandbar with the tide rising.

Still, the oar was his best hope for forcing the slats apart. Jonno set one foot on the slat behind Pip's trapped leg, wrapped his left hand around the slat in front of it and pulled upward. At the same time he pushed down on the oar with his right hand. With a sudden lurch, the oar grated downward, the blade striking through the slats to the sand beneath.

"Steady now, Pip. Right where you are. Stay!"

Sweat chilled by fog and the salty wind dripped into Jonno's eyes, but he couldn't stop now. He wanted desperately to hurry, but he must be careful. Moving slowly, slowly to avoid throwing pressure against Pip's leg, he stepped up on the lower slat to test the old wood's pliancy. One foot up and then the other. He was grateful now for the wet sneakers gripping the splintery wood, as the slat gave way under his feet. Pip whimpered and wriggled. His leg slid part way to freedom. But only part way.

Risky though it was, he would have to try using the oar as a lever—and he would have to hope that the lobster pot and not the oar would give way first, for it would be a long swim to shore in the strengthening current.

Jonno grasped the oar's handle with both hands, dug his left foot into the sand, and braced his right against the lower slat, which had begun to weaken.

"Okay, Pip, we've got to move together. One, two, three, Pip—go!"

On "go!" Jonno pulled upward on the oar with all his might. Wood cracked. Pippin made a startled lurch backward and tumbled free. Jonno's thrust threw him backward into a heap on the sand. His head felt like a spinning top, and his leg throbbed where the oar's handle had landed on it, but he'd worry about all that later. The oar was whole.

Beside Jonno, Pip crouched low, licking his paw. Jonno felt gently along the dog's leg. His paw was bleeding from a cut here and a torn pad there, but no dangling limpness warned of a broken bone.

Anyway, this was no place to recuperate. Fog clouded all the seaward fringes of Jonno's vision, and the skiff was completely afloat. "Nae man can tether time nor tide," rumbled Rob's voice in Jonno's memory. They had to get moving.

"I hate to do this to you, Pip," said Jonno, "but you've got to try to walk, 'cause there's no way I can carry you." He scrambled to his feet, snatched the oar away from the broken slats of the lobster pot, and set off at a jog toward the boat, not looking back until he heard Pip move behind him. Pip followed slowly, looking reproachful, limping on his injured leg. But he can do it, thought Jonno with immense relief. The leg's not broken!

Even so, with his paw injured and the current strengthening, Pip couldn't be turned loose to swim to safety. Suspicious though he was of boats, he would have to be rowed ashore.

Water swirled around Jonno's calves as he hauled in the skiff and freed the anchor. Pip had to be poked, pulled, and prodded, but at last Jonno maneuvered him into the boat's stern and climbed in after him.

Jonno fixed the oars in the locks and looked around quickly to get his bearings. Before him, fog curtained the far side of the sandbar; behind him, fog drifted across the dunes' backs and into the cove. They had to hurry.

"Nae man can tether." He had to stand up to push the skiff away from the sandbar, for it rode much lower in the water with a large, soggy dog in its stern. "Time nor tide." I'll check my direction once, and then just row like mad for shore, Jonno told himself. Turning around all the time would only cost him rhythm, time, and energy. Through the veils that ran ahead of the fogbank into the cove, he could just make out the cluster of masts that lay behind the skiff's mooring. He steadied the little boat's bow toward that spot as best he could, faced Pip, who looked as nervous as Jonno felt, and pulled away on the oars.

Dip, pull, lift; dip, pull, lift. Jonno tried to make himself concentrate on the rhythm and ignore the burning knot between his shoulder blades where his muscles were protesting all this rowing. Dip, pull, lift. The incoming tide was a boon in one way, for it would help to push him shoreward—but a hazard in another, for as the water rose it grew more swift and choppy.

Dip, pull, lift. Jonno watched the fog advance toward the near edge of the sandbar, and reckoned they must have covered some third of the distance back to shore. On an impulse, he turned to check his guesswork and froze, his rhythm on the oars forgotten. Far off to his left, some roofs and chimneys on the bluff floated like ghosts above the mist, but the shore behind him had disappeared. While he dipped, pulled, and lifted, staring at his soggy dog and his own soggy sneakers, the fog had overrun the edges of the cove. He felt colder suddenly and swallowed hard. "No time to panic, Ayres," he told himself aloud. But the words were muffled as if by cotton batting, and he realized that he wasn't cold from shock alone. Like the fog now blurring the last edges of the sandbar, the fog on shore was coming at him. Jonno shivered as the first clammy veil slid across the skiff's bow.

Gripping his neglected oars, Jonno felt the skiff slipping sideways into the troughs of the following sea. He twisted frantically, peering in one direction and then another, but even the roofs and chimneys disappeared as he strained to keep them in sight. His landmarks were gone.

He fought down panic. He should keep rowing, but which way? Just staying with the current would take him ashore at the water's whim, not necessarily by the mooring for the borrowed boat. And anyway, currents shifted. He had heard stories of boaters struggling for hours in fog only to find they'd been going in circles. If the wind strengthened and the waves came up much more, the skiff might capsize. And the currents were getting stronger all the time.

He wouldn't let himself think about that. The skiff rocked in the trough of more determined waves, and Jonno dug with the oar he guessed was on his seaward side, hoping he had pulled the boat's nose back toward the beach.

Thoughts chased one another through his mind, and only one was hopeful. His father might find the note on the fishhook and come looking for him. He could yell, in case that happened. Then he could row with the current and yell some more.

It was hard to row and yell at the same time, so Jonno lifted his oars again, turned his head, and hollered, *"Hellllloooooo."* But the wind seemed to snatch the cry away, the fog to smother it. The word died in his throat and choking panic took its place. "Nae man can tether time nor tide," and he and Pip were truly at their mercy. He had never felt so helpless. Nor so alone.

And then he heard the music.

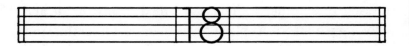

The wisp of piping wove through the fog behind him and was blown away by the next gust of wind from the sea.

Jonno's breath caught in his throat. His hands locked on the oars.

There it was again, and gone again in half a minute.

This was more frustrating than trying to hear the World Series through a barrage of radio static—and frightening, like a nightmare of drowning and straining toward a lifeline that was always out of reach. The skiff slid sideways in insistent swells, while he sat as still as anyone could be in a tossing boat, trying to sift the sound of pipes from the sounds of wind and water.

Why Rob, hurting and angry as he'd been a day ago, would be on the beach in such weather—that was more than Jonno could imagine. But if the piping was real, he could follow it like a lifeline, let it draw him safely to the beach. So, more than he had ever concentrated on an incoming pitch, more intently than he had ever listened to a coach's game plan, Jonno concentrated now on that trickle of melody.

He pulled the skiff out of the waves' trough again, guiding it by the memory of the last faint, reedy strains he thought he'd heard. Dip, pull, lift. Dip, pull, lift. "You've a good ear, Jonno," Rob had told him once. But what if this had nothing to do with his ear, but was all in his mind? I could be cracking up, he thought abruptly, with a pang of fresh fear that snatched his breath again. Once before when fog hung on the dunes he had watched the piper pass and wondered if he were a specter. He'd heard enough scary stories to know that fog distorted sound as well as sight. What if this ragged music was like a mirage in the desert, an illusion wanderers followed only to be doomed or disappointed?

Maybe his first instinct for survival had been right, and he must simply row and yell. Dip, pull, lift. Dip, pull, lift. The breeze had held brisk for long minutes, and Jonno's hands were cold on the oars. He lifted the oars from the water and was turning his head to holler again, when Pippin caught his attention for the first time since the fog had closed in. Since they had left the sandbar, Pip had huddled in the skiff's stern, head bent over his torn paw. Now his ears were up and he peered steadily in one direction. Clearly Pip was listening, so Jonno closed his mouth and listened, too.

The wind dropped slightly. Rising, beckoning came again the wail of the Great Highland Warpipe. Too noisy for a mirage. Real. With a tune he now could recognize as "Scotland the Brave." Far too cheerful for a ghost.

Jonno dug deep with one oar and pulled the skiff's bow toward the sound of the pipes. Dip, pull, lift. There never had been any explaining Rob, so he'd follow the music and stop telling himself it couldn't be there. Right now, all Jonno wanted was to get ashore before it stopped.

Over his shoulder he still saw nothing but fog, yet the music grew louder, resisting the wind's efforts to blow it away again. "Skye Boat Song." "Speed, bonnie boat, like a bird on the wing." Almost as if the piper were cheering him on.

Whatever brought Rob to the cove, Jonno found he couldn't help rejoicing in the sound. "Carry the lad that's born to be king over the sea to Skye." It lilted through his cocoon of fog and lifted his spirits. The knot between his shoulders was tighter than ever, but Jonno realized with surprise that he was smiling. "Enough to make my grandmother rally round the flag." Well, enough to keep a worn-out oarsman rowing. Enough to draw a boy and dog to safety. Jonno grinned again as the song swelled and stopped.

In the sudden hush, wind breathed, water lapped, and behind him came the dull clunk of metal striking metal. Jonno turned and saw the red sailboat called *Dragonfly* rocking just yards ahead, nudged into its nearest neighbor by the sea. Not far beyond would be the place where he had found the skiff. He felt as if a large weight had been lifted from his chest. If he could avoid doing something dumb for the next five minutes, they might even land at the right spot. No matter now if the music stopped and Rob moved on. After yesterday, Jonno wouldn't know what to say to him anyway.

With one oar and then the other, Jonno nosed the skiff between boats' moorings. He thought he could see now where the water ended. Since the tide had just turned, the place where he'd found the skiff would still be beyond the water line. "Pippin—stay!" Jonno shipped the oars, picked up the bow line, and clambered over the skiff's side into waist-deep flowing water. His sneakers sank in silt as he began to haul the skiff aground. And just then came another burst of music.

For some reason Jonno couldn't fathom, Rob had not moved on after all. And now he was playing "All the Bluebonnets Are Over the Border" as if a whole regiment were right on his heels. Close. Very close.

The skiff struck bottom, and Pippin began to scramble out more clumsily than usual. "For pete's sake, Pip, hold on a minute!" Jonno dropped the rope and tried to bolster Pip's front end as the big dog dropped onto the sand with a splatter. Then he watched Pip limp off toward the music, ears alert. Jonno struggled with the urge he'd had since the first day on the bluff—to follow the sound. Two things stopped him. The need to secure the borrowed boat. And fear of Rob's not wanting to see him.

So he took his time beaching the skiff. Up the slope of soaking sand he pulled the bow and pushed the stern, hard work for screaming muscles. Finally he staggered up the ridge of sand from which he'd dragged the anchor, and at last the struggle was over. Jonno's knees were wobbly, but he had to get on. Find Pip and get him home. Which meant finding Rob, literally facing the music.

"Bluebonnets" ended and as suddenly began again. Jonno retraced his steps to the water's edge through fog so thick he could see little more than the skiff's length in any direction. Then it was easy to follow Pip's saucerlike paw prints, which led toward the boats clustered in the marsh grass on the inner rim of the cove. But even without the trail, it would have been impossible now to miss the music.

He still didn't know what to say to Rob. He should probably tell him that the piping had accidentally saved the day. He should probably apologize for having said too much yesterday and made Rob angry. But now that he was nearly on top of the music, filled with it again, he felt that apologies were not appropriate. He was sorry he had made Rob angry, but he still believed the argument that had raised the anger. What was there to lose? He'd echo Rob again, if he got the chance, about the need for taking risks and chasing dreams.

Suddenly Pip was squarely in Jonno's path, crouching and wagging in his usual confused reaction to pipe music. A few more steps brought Jonno to Pip's side, and far enough through the fog to see Rob at last.

He had bundled himself into a well-frayed sailing parka and tied some gauze around the outstretched calf of his sore leg, but otherwise Rob perched on the overturned rowboat as nonchalantly as if he were tuning up for a parade in the year's finest weather. His face looked drawn but peaceful, and as Jonno appeared Rob cocked an eyebrow at him and sent him a wink above the blowpipe.

Rob finished "Bluebonnets" with a flourish, swung down the pipes, and regarded Jonno gravely. Then almost solemnly, still sitting with his bandaged leg thrown across the boat's planks, he held out his right hand in a gesture that was half-salute. It reminded Jonno oddly of a scene showing King Arthur knighting Sir Galahad, and made him feel as shy and uncertain as he had the first morning on the Farnums' porch. But it was a gesture of command, so Jonno stepped forward and put his slightly shaky, clammy hand into Rob's dry, warm, steady one.

A twinkle leaped in Rob's gray eyes. "Just as I thought, it was Jonathan Ayres," he said. "That was some rescue!"

Rob was actually there, looking as natural and serene as the driftwood spar that marked the path to the bluff. And he had been there for quite a while, almost as if he were standing watch for Jonno.

You have to take a chance, he heard as clearly as if Rob had said it again aloud. "Rob," said Jonno, in a voice that refused to stay coolly even, "I'm not sure we'd have made it in, if you hadn't been here!"

Rob punctuated a shrug with a skeptical sound and shook his head. "I referred to your rescue of Pip, of course. But I did hope the pipes would serve, lacking a foghorn, or I'd not be down here in weather thick as week-old soup."

Jonno felt as if his brain were hung up between bases. "You mean you're here because of me? Not out for a walk?"

Rob smiled—not the wide grin like a boy's that lit his face like lightning, but a gentler smile that lifted just the corners of his mouth and deepened the crinkles at the corners of his eyes. He laid his free hand on Jonno's shoulder. "I admit I've done a lot of piping in weather a duck would sneer at, but to do it when my leg is actin' up, I need good reason. Like a mate in distress." He shook Jonno's shoulder playfully, but his eyes were shinier than usual.

Then he threw back his shoulders and cleared his throat. "I found your note, Jonno. I woke up this morning feelin' like the village ogre, and decided I'd best get over to your gram's and mend my fences."

Close your stupid mouth, Ayres, thought Jonno fiercely, but not before Rob had caught his look of amazement.

"Look here." Rob chuckled. "I know ye're astonished to hear I'm not perfect, but I'm plain sorry I was such a grouch yesterday. It wasn't you I was mad at, o' course; it was myself. And time. And it's hard not to get edgy when outargued by yer own philosophy. Anyway—off to yer grandmother's house I went, and found only yer note there, so I headed here on the chance I'd find you searching. I only meant to hail you from yer spot of wild surmise up there and bring you with me while I wrapped myself around a cup of hot tea. But I got there just in time to see the wee boat fadin' in the fog, and decided I'd better stand by. Sort of a noisy rear guard. Surely a slow one. I'd have got the music goin' sooner, but it took some time to get the blasted leg down all those stairs."

Jonno shook his head. "I can't believe you went to all that trouble."

"Hush!" Rob's grin flashed then. "I said I'd had experience with landings. I'm glad it was enough to bring you in."

"It was enough," said Jonno, and he smiled, too. "Almost enough to make Gram rally 'round the flag."

Thoughts spun through a silence while they just looked at one another. "Enough," said Jonno finally with a sureness that surprised himself, "to make me think I'd like to be a piper."

This time the smile that started in Rob's eyes spread steadily from ear to ear. "I did have hopes." Rob nodded toward the faded knapsack perched beside him. "There's things for you here. That practice chanter, only slightly

160

the worse for yer wild delivery, and a beaten old book I used when I was just beginnin'."

"But how did you know . . ."

"I didn't. I just wanted you to have 'em. I've another thing to tell you, Jonno," Rob added, "before we try those steps again. While you take yer hairy friend there to his doctor, I'll be gettin' ready to go off to mine."

Jonno's eye fell on a knobby cane propped against the rowboat's stern. He still felt that he was playing a game without having learned the signals. "You mean you're going to let the doctors fix your leg?"

Rob gave him a level look and nodded.

"Rob, that's great! But yesterday I thought you'd never change your mind!"

"You changed it," Rob said. "You, and yer dog, and all my own words that you've thrown back at me." Rob tossed his head toward the invisible bluff and the path to the Farnums'. "I got to thinkin' last night, as I lounged about with the Farnums fussin' over me, that in my thousand years of knockin' about alone I'd lost sight of how important friends are. For just one reason, a friend can tell you things you don't want to tell yourself. As you did yesterday."

Jonno opened his mouth, but Rob went right on. "So I come out today, convinced again we're right to tell each other that there's no use livin' if you won't take risks. And find you settin' off for nowhere in a boat like a matchbox. Riskin' yer very neck. Confirmin' all my preachin's that I didn't want to practice.

"So, aye, I'm goin' back to that hospital to see if they can really get me back in tune. Give us a hand then, Jonno."

And Rob became businesslike, rearranging his legs and gathering up his knapsack.

In spite of the wind and his soggy state, Jonno had a light, warm place in his solar plexus where the leaden hollow had been before. "Do you mean you're leaving right away?" he asked.

"Aye. They've a place for me tomorrow. It's not as if I'm gettin' younger by the minute, and they can't really tell how long their magic's goin' to take."

"Nae man can tether time nor tide," Jonno thought again. He held out a hand to help Rob stand, and only as Rob grasped it he realized what was happening. There was no way to know if Rob would be back before the Ayreses' vacation ended. The truth was he might never see Rob again.

Carefully, Rob pulled himself erect. Then he looked intently into Jonno's face and handed him the knapsack. "Ye're welcome to the rucksack, too; I'll not be hikin' for a while."

"Thanks, Rob," Jonno said unsteadily.

"Jonathan Ayres," said Rob, in the same stern voice he'd used before for promises. "We're goin' to meet again. And when I tell you somethin' . . ."

"I know, I can believe it." Jonno swallowed and brushed away some moisture on his cheek that wasn't fog. "But it's hard not to feel sad, Rob, when I don't know how we'll ever see each other."

"I'll write—I will!—and tell you what the medicine men are up to," Rob declared, setting his arm around Jonno's shoulders. "And here's a thought from Robbie Burns you might remember."

"I know," said Jonno softly. " 'No man can tether time nor tide.' "

"No," said Rob. "Another one." As gray and faintly shining as the fog and sea, his eyes held Jonno's. " 'Fate still has blest me with a friend,' " he said.

At the top of the forty-two steps they stopped on the splintery bench to rest Rob's leg. Comforted by Rob's arm still laid across his shoulders, Jonno was cold and bone-weary, but not ready to leave Rob. Not ready to go home.

He'd never forget this afternoon. But he wished he could throw off the blanket of fog and see the whole sweep of the inlet. Not the sunny, postcard image that he carried in his memory all year long, but this precise scene of gray swells, cold sands, and lurking lobster trap, with a small blue skiff just coming afloat near the catboat called *Dragonfly*.

It was eerie to think that in an hour or so the tide would cover the sandbar, maybe even bury the lobster trap for another year or ten, if the currents were strong enough. The blue skiff would bob innocently at anchor just as it had at the last high tide. No trace of his adventure would remain. Once Pip's paw healed, Jonno supposed even Pip would forget it. It would all be gone except for what was stamped upon his memory—a shroud of fog torn open by a shaft of melody.

It would make a good story, as good as some of his father's. Would he tell it someday to a boy of his own? If he had a boy he would, Jonno thought—and others, of the first day in the fog and the wild ride to Rafferty's. Not so much because he and his boy would laugh together then, but because, as Rob once said, it was how he'd keep Rob with him.

Pippin whimpered patiently.

"Jonno." Rob thumped his shoulder gently. "Pip hurts, and time is goin'. I dread the partin', too, but you both could stand a rub and a bowl of something warm. Just scribble down yer address, now, before we go."

Jonno's fingers were stiff around the stubby pencil, and his toes were beginning to be sore as well as cold. Wet sand grated in his sneakers, but he was too tired to take them off and carry them. Since he didn't trust his voice, he simply hoisted Rob's knapsack onto his own shoulder, as they stiffly rose and turned for home.

"Jonno-oh!"

They had nearly reached the hedgerows' end and the road that led to the Farnums' when Alison's whoop stopped them. Scattering pebbles down the dirt road from the main crossing, she flew out of the fog, his father loping along behind her.

"And Pippin! Boy, were we worried!"

Still spouting exclamation points, she charged at Jonno like a runner stealing home, and threw her arms around his waist. She was warm and for once she smelled more of pine needles than of bubble gum; her cheeks were pink instead of white as they'd been when he snapped at her yesterday, and to his surprise Jonno found himself hugging her back. He might tell her the whole story, too, he thought. She was worth taking a chance on.

Phil Ayres came on more slowly, smiling with relief, his eyes searching Jonno's and Rob's faces. He managed to turn a tousling of Jonno's hair into a quick hug before he faced Rob.

"You have to be Rob Loud," he said. "And I'm Phil Ayres."

Rob's gray gaze swung to meet his father's. "I'm glad t' meet you, Philip Ayres—and sorry for the timing. I'd've liked to know a man who can raise a lad like Jonno."

Phil Ayres's answer was spoken across a long handshake. "I'm sorry if that means you're leaving. I'm sure that I'd have liked that, too."

Jonno watched the men's eyes, gray and hazel, and in spite of Gram and Grace Goodspeed, believed what his father said.

"Perhaps another year." Rob's *r*'s rumbled. "Well, Jonno." It was a statement, not a beginning. "Good luck with those." Rob gestured at the knapsack that held the book and chanter. He held out a hand to Jonno, and then abruptly pulled him close. It was a clumsy hug, involving the knapsack, the pipes, the slipping, knobbly cane, and the smell of fog, salt, and tobacco. But it was like another promise, and it made Jonno feel better.

For seconds more Rob held him with a look and the hand that didn't grasp the pipes and cane. "We'll take a cup of kindness yet." He nodded and sparks danced again in the gray eyes. "Who knows—maybe at Cowal!"

"Right," said Jonno. What was it Rob had told him, the night they came back from Rafferty's? "Good luck with the dragons."

Rob was gone, in the mist, by the time Phil Ayres had knelt to look at Pippin's paw. "I'm sure he'll be okay, but we'll take him to Dr. Hopkins just to be sure," said Jonno's father. "Tell me what happened, Jonno."

Brief. Be brief. There'd be time later for details, for all the signs the tide was covering and the feelings he might yet keep to himself.

"He got his foot caught in an old lobster pot out on the sandbar. The tide was coming in, so I had to go and get him. In the little blue skiff that's near the *Dragonfly*."

His father looked up quickly in surprise. "You mean you were alone?"

Jonno nodded, and more questions flared in his father's eyes.

"And you had no trouble with the fog?"

"Um." For a heart-stopping instant, Jonno was back in the boat, in a fogbank pierced by piping. "Rob read my note and went down to the beach with his pipes. His music led me in."

Alison's eyes were round and admiring. "Jonno, weren't you scared?"

Jonno shrugged. Then he looked at her directly and nodded. "Yes. But I was able to follow the music."

Still soothing Pippin with his hands, Jonno's father gave him a long, level look. "You did well, Jonno," he said quietly.

Jonno hesitated. The childhood impulse to keep the moon shell in his pocket was still with him, but he was certain now that Rob's friendship would bear any sort of scrutiny. And then there was the business of the pipes. If he wanted to "have a go at them," as Rob would say, he would have to tell his parents, and maybe the perfect moment was any time like this, when Kate and Gram were somewhere else. Besides, as Rob said, if something was worthwhile, it was worth taking chances for. He looked at his father, clearly full of relief and pride, and knew there'd be other stories of today besides his own. And that it was time he took some chances with his father, too.

"Dad," he said, "there's something else I want to tell you, before we get back to Gram's. I want to learn to play the pipes."

His father looked at him with the kind of light in his eyes that would always remind Jonno of Rob Loud.

"I thought you might," was all his father said.